A ROGUE'S FLOWER

A ROGUE'S FLOWER

PROLOGUE

"Elsbeth?"

Miss Elsbeth Blakely, daughter to some unknown persons and nothing more than an orphan, turned her head to see Miss Skelton enter the room, her thin figure and skeletal appearance matching her name perfectly.

"Yes, Miss Skelton?" Elsbeth asked, getting to her feet as she knew she was expected to, given that this was the lady in charge of the House for Girls. "What can I do for you?"

Miss Skelton, her black hair tied back into a tight bun, gave a small disparaging sniff. "What are you doing in the schoolroom, Elsbeth? The dinner gong has sounded, has it not?"

Elsbeth did not back down, nor feel ashamed of her tardiness. "I have every intention of coming to the dining hall the moment I have finished my letter," she replied, calmly. "After all, was it not you yourself who told me that I was to leave this place just as soon as I could?" She tilted her head just a little, mousey brown curls tipping across her forehead as she did so. Her hair had always been the bane of her life, for she had such tight curls that it was almost impossible to keep them neat and tidy as she was expected to do.

Miss Skelton sniffed again. "That is no excuse, Elsbeth. I expect better from you."

Elsbeth sighed inwardly, aware that Miss Skelton was almost always disappointed with her. Ever since she could remember, Miss Skelton had been a tall, imposing figure that gave her nothing but disparaging and cutting remarks, designed to bring down her confidence. Elsbeth had, in fact, learned how to stand against Miss Skelton's venomous words, shutting down her emotions and closeting away her heart whenever the lady spoke.

"May I ask what letter it is you are writing?" Miss Skelton asked, her hands now clasped in front of her. Her long, grey dress with its high collar that hid most of her neck hung on her like a shroud, giving her an almost death-like appearance that Elsbeth hated so much.

"I have been responding to advertisements regarding governesses," Elsbeth replied, with a slight lift of her chin. "Mrs. Banks has encouraged me in this and I intend to find a position very soon. I do hope that you will give me the references I require." She lifted one eyebrow, a slight challenge in her voice as she waited for Miss Skelton to reply. Mrs. Banks, the lady who taught the girls everything from elocution to grammar, had encouraged Elsbeth in her hopes of making a life for herself outside of the Smithfield House for Girls. Mrs. Banks told her that she had all the knowledge and ability required to become a governess. In a recent spat with Miss Skelton, Elsbeth had been urged to leave the House for Girls as soon as she was able. Miss Skelton pointed out how frustrated she was that she could not throw Elsbeth out on her ear; the two things had come together to encourage Elsbeth to indeed depart. What she required of Miss Skelton was a reference to whichever one of her potential employers wrote back to her with further enquiry.

"I suppose I must," Miss Skelton replied, her voice thin. "If it means that I can get you out of this place, then I will do all I can to help you."

Elsbeth found herself smiling, feeling as though she had won victory. "Thank you, Miss Skelton. It is much appreciated, I am sure." Turning her back on the lady, she sat down again and continued to compose her letter, hearing Miss Skelton's mutter of frustration before she left the room.

Breathing a small sigh of relief, Elsbeth let her pen drift over the page, writing the same words she had written on three other occasions. Her desire to become a governess was growing with every day that she had to spend here. Even though it was the only home she had ever known, it was slowly beginning to suffocate her.

The Smithfield House for Girls was right next to the bustling Smithfield Market, but was in direct contrast to the happiness and warmth that came from there. Elsbeth often spent time looking out of her window to the market place, finding her heart filled with both happiness and pain, wishing that she could have the same joy that was in the faces of so many of those who came to the market.

They laughed and smiled more than anyone ever did in the House for Girls, mostly due to the fact that Miss Skelton was neither happy nor joyful.

Lost in thought for a moment, Elsbeth looked up from her page and let her gaze drift towards the window. Whilst her life had not been altogether bad thus far, the question about where she had come from and why she was here had always dogged her mind. Miss Skelton had never said a word, other than to state that her living allowances had been paid for – and continued to be paid for – year after year. That was why she could never throw Elsbeth out onto the street, since money was sent specifically for Elsbeth's upkeep. Elsbeth could still remember the day she had asked Miss Skelton who sent the money, only for the door to be shut in her face. That had been the day she had begun to dislike Miss Skelton intensely. Elsbeth was frustrated that the woman would not give her any information despite seeing the it upset her to have no knowledge of her birth.

Elsbeth had quietly resigned herself to the fact that she would never know, not unless her father or mother came looking for her. It was an agony that would never fully disappear from her heart, the pain of not understanding why she had been sent here as a baby. Why had her parents had turned her over to Miss Skelton instead of keeping her to raise themselves? She did not understand why Miss Skelton would not speak to her about the matter, did not understand why she would not even explain why she would not do so. That, however, was a burden Elsbeth knew she simply had to bear. Miss Skelton was not about to change her mind, in the same way that she was not about to become a warm and kind-hearted lady who cared about the charges in the House she ran.

That being said, Elsbeth knew that most of the girls here were from noblemen or gentlemen who had chosen to have a tryst outside of wedlock or outside their marriages. It was more than obvious that this was the case, for the girls were trained in all manner of gentle arts, instead of simply being fed and given a place to sleep as they would have done in the poorhouse. There were standards here, standards that both she and the others were expected to meet. Most of them might never know their fathers nor their mothers, but at least their chance at a decent life was much greater than if they'd been left at the poorhouse. There were varying choices for them in their futures – although most would become governesses or teachers in places such as these. Some would become seamstresses, others perhaps marry. Elsbeth winced as she recalled that the annual ball was due to take place in two days' time – a chance for the girls who were out to take part in a small gathering where gentlemen in the lower classes could attend in case they were in need of a wife.... or, perhaps, a mistress. She was revolted at the thought, her eyes closing tightly as she fought against the urge to run away from it all. Being now of age, she had no other choice but to attend, even though she was already responding to advertisements for governesses. Whilst Miss Skelton wanted to be rid of her, Elsbeth knew that it would be in any way she could, which included the ball and a potential husband.

Not that the gentlemen who attended were in any

way nobility. They were mostly baronets, knights, and the like, who were looking for a wife who could fulfill all their requirements whilst still being of decent standing. In addition, Elsbeth knew that many of the girls had a large dowry set aside for them, although none knew from where it had come. That was what brought such gentlemen to the ball, for even though there might be some murmuring over marriages to girls from the Smithfield House for Girls, a gentleman could overlook it should there be a large enough dowry.

Elsbeth had not thought to ask about herself, and was, therefore, quite unaware of any dowry she might have. Perhaps there would be a way for her to hide from most of the gentlemen on the evening of the ball, regardless of whether she had a dowry or not. She did not wish to marry. She wanted to experience life outside of this place, a life where she could earn her own living and make her own way if she chose. Marriage was just another four walls around her, keeping her in line.

Sighing heavily, Elsbeth finished writing her letter, sanded it carefully and then folded it up, ready to be posted.

"Please," she whispered, holding the letter carefully in her hand. "Please, let this be the way out of here. Let me find a new life, far away from Smithfield, London and Miss Skelton. Please." Closing her eyes tightly, she sent her prayer heavenwards before rising from her chair and making her way to the dining room. All she could do now was wait.

CHAPTER ONE

The following afternoon found Elsbeth finishing her embroidery piece, feeling rather pleased with herself. Embroidery had not come naturally to her and yet here she was, finishing off her final piece.

"Wonderful, Elsbeth!" Mrs. Banks exclaimed, coming to sit by her. "You should be very pleased with your work."

"Thank you, Mrs. Banks," Elsbeth replied, with a chuckle. "Although I will say that I do not understand how anyone can find any kind of enjoyment from such a thing."

Mrs. Banks smiled back, her plump face warm and friendly. "Then I should tell you that I do not particularly enjoy it myself, but it is a useful skill to have when one is seeking a husband."

Elsbeth suppressed a shudder. "Thank goodness I am not doing so."

Mrs. Banks nodded slowly. "The ball is tomorrow night. Did Miss Skelton speak to you about it?"

A niggle of worry tugged at Elsbeth's mind. "No, she did not. Why?"

For a moment, Mrs. Banks looked away, her lips thinning and Elsbeth felt herself grow tense.

"You have a large dowry, Elsbeth. I am surprised Miss Skelton has not spoken to you about this before now."

Elsbeth shook her head, firmly. "I do not care. I will not marry."

"I know, I know," Mrs. Banks said softly, putting one gentle hand on Elsbeth's. "But Miss Skelton will be sharing that news with whichever gentlemen show an interest in you at the ball. You must be prepared for that."

Elsbeth felt ice grip her heart, making her skin prickle. "I do not want to marry," she whispered, her embroidery now sitting uselessly on her lap, completely forgotten. "I know Miss Skelton wishes to get rid of me, but I cannot bring myself to preen in front of eligible gentlemen in the hope of matrimony! I want a life for myself."

Mrs. Banks gave her a small reassuring smile, one hand reaching out to rest on her shoulder. "And I am sure you will receive a return to your letters very soon," she replied, calmly, "but you must be aware of what Miss Skelton intends to do. Your dowry is very large, Elsbeth. You have clearly come from a wealthy family."

Putting her head in her hands, Elsbeth battled frustration. So much money, just out of reach. With it, she could do whatever she pleased, set up a life for herself wherever she wanted.

"Although...."

Her head jerked up as she saw Mrs. Banks look from one place to the next, her eyes a little concerned.

"Although?" Elsbeth repeated, encouraging the lady. "Although what, Mrs. Banks?"

Mrs. Banks paused for a moment before shaking her head. "Never mind. It is not something I should say."

Knowing that Mrs. Banks was the closest thing she had to a friend, Elsbeth reached across and took her hand. "Please, Mrs. Banks, tell me whatever it was you were going to say. I feel so lost already. Anything you can tell me will help." Her blue eyes searched Mrs. Banks' face, desperate to know what the lady was holding back.

"I should not be telling you this, Elsbeth," Mrs. Banks replied quietly, "but I have seen how miserable you are here and how Miss Skelton treats you. I am sorry for that. You are a free spirit and she, being as tight-laced as she is, does not understand that. She has never wanted to nurture you, she has simply wanted to contain you, and I cannot hold with that."

A lump in her throat, Elsbeth squeezed Mrs. Banks' hand. "I know," she replied, quietly. "I have valued your teaching and your friendship over the years."

Mrs. Banks drew in a long breath, her shoulders settling as she came to a decision. "As have I," she said, with a great deal more firmness. "Then I shall tell you the truth about your dowry. If you do not marry before you are twenty-one years of age, then the dowry, in all its entirety, goes to you."

Elsbeth gaped at her, her world slowly beginning to spin around her.

"Just think of it, Elsbeth," Mrs. Banks continued

softly, her voice warm. "You need only be a governess for three or four years before you will be truly free. If you are careful, I believe you will have enough to live on for the rest of your days."

Elsbeth could not breathe, her chest constricting. She could hardly believe it, could hardly take it all in, and yet she knew that what Mrs. Banks was saying was the truth. She would not lie to her.

"Why has Miss Skelton never spoken to me about this?" she asked hoarsely, as Mrs. Banks squeezed her hand. "I could have stayed here until...."

"You have answered your own question," Mrs. Banks replied, sadly. "Miss Skelton wants you gone from her establishment and she thought that, in telling you the truth, you would be filled with the urge to remain. There will be funds aplenty until you reach the age of twenty-one, for I am certain that Miss Skelton told me that whoever it is that pays for your board here would do so until either you are wed, or you are twenty-one."

Elsbeth shook her head, fervently. "That cannot be the case. Miss Skelton told me that I must find a place soon as the money that pays for me will soon cease."

"Another lie, I'm afraid," Mrs. Banks said softly, as Elsbeth felt her heart break all over again. "For whatever reason, Miss Skelton is desperate to have you gone from this place. She forbade me to speak of it to you but I knew I could not keep the truth from you. It is too great a truth to have hidden away. It would have been wrong of me to keep it to myself."

Elsbeth drew in breath after breath, her mind whirling as she tried her best to think calmly and clearly about all that had been revealed to her. Miss Skelton had always disliked her but to hide such an enormous truth from her cut Elsbeth to the bone.

"You will have your freedom one day soon," Mrs. Banks promised, putting her arm around her as Elsbeth leaned into her shoulder, just as she might have done with her mother. "Just a few more years."

Trying not to cry, Elsbeth buried her face into Mrs. Banks shoulder. "I do not think I can endure any more time here."

"Then be a governess," Mrs. Banks replied, with a small shrug. "Do whatever you wish, whatever you can until you reach twenty-one. And do not marry a gentleman, whatever you do. I know Miss Skelton is hopeful, but I would encourage you to find a way not to attend the ball tomorrow evening or, at the very least, make yourself as inconspicuous as possible."

Caught by a sudden thought, Elsbeth lifted her head. "You will not get yourself into trouble with Miss Skelton over this? I would hate for you to lose your position."

Mrs. Banks smiled softly, patting Elsbeth's cheek. "You are so caring, my dear. And no, so long as you do not reveal it to her then I think all will be well. Besides which, I do not think that Miss Skelton would dare fire me from this position – for who would she find to replace me? Her reputation as a hard woman, with little care or consideration for anyone but herself is well known." She tipped her head, her eyes alive with mirth. "Do you truly think that she would be able to find another worker with any kind of ease?"

Elsbeth had to laugh, despite her confusion and astonishment. "No, I do not think she would."

"Then you need not worry," Mrs. Banks replied, with a broad smile. "Now, off with you. Go and see if there are any letters that need to be posted so that you might take a turn about the London streets. It might help you think a little more clearly."

"I am rather overwhelmed," Elsbeth admitted, shaking her head. "Thank you for telling me so much, Mrs. Banks. I am indebted to you."

Mrs. Banks smiled again, her eyes suddenly filling with tears. "I shall miss you, when it comes time for you to leave, Elsbeth," she said quietly. "You will promise to write to me, whatever happens?"

Bending down to kiss Mrs. Banks' cheeks, Elsbeth pressed her hands for a moment. "Of course I will, Mrs. Banks. You have made my life so much better here and I will always be grateful for your love and your care for me. Thank you."

CHAPTER TWO

Whilst there were no letters to be sent, there was, according to the housekeeper who did the bidding of Miss Skelton, a need for Elsbeth to adorn the front of the House for Girls with flowers. Apparently, it was a reminder to all the gentlemen who had been invited that the ball was to happen tomorrow evening. Elsbeth did not quite understand given that so many of them had already sent their replies to confirm that, yes, they were to attend tomorrow evening's festivities.

Regardless, Elsbeth did as the housekeeper directed without making even a murmur of protest, thinking that to be outside instead of kept within the House would possibly give her the time she needed to think about all that Mrs. Banks had said. She was in no doubt that Miss Skelton had not said as much to her as regards her dowry and the wonderful age of twenty-one when she would attain her freedom, simply because she did not want Elsbeth to remain in the House for Girls. There had always been something about Elsbeth that Miss Skelton disliked, and now she was making it even more apparent that she did not care for her in the slightest. Whilst Elsbeth knew that she was, as Mrs. Banks had said, a free spirit flying in the face of Miss Skelton's harsh and firmly aligned ways, there had never been any other explanation as to why the lady had taken such a dislike to her. From her earliest memories, Elsbeth could recall Miss Skelton being dismissive and disinterested in her whilst being a *little* more jovial to the other girls. That had only bred anger and resentment in Elsbeth, who had grown more than a little frustrated with the lady's continued dislike of her; so, in her own way, she had done all she could to battle against the lady's hostility, to the point that she knew exactly what to say and do to bring her the most frustration.

Perhaps it was a little childish, Elsbeth reflected, as she picked up the basket which held the brightly colored flowers and the string with which she could tie bunches to the railings that surrounded the House for Girls. Then again, she had been a child for a very long time and only in the last few years had begun the journey towards adulthood. Miss Skelton had never changed, and Elsbeth had felt herself shrinking away from her more and more. She often sought the friendship and understanding of Mrs. Banks, a mother figure to all the orphan girls, and did not think she would have survived life here without her.

But now she had to consider what path to take. She *could* remain here until she was twenty-one, in order to come into her fortune, but that would mean over three years of Miss Skelton's dark looks and embittered words. To continue her quest to become a governess seemed the most likely path to take, for then she could simply give up that life when the time came. What would she do then? Where would she go? It was all so unexpected and yet Elsbeth was filled with a delicious excitement. To finally be free, to finally be able to build her own life....it was so near and yet so very far away.

Walking outside, Elsbeth paused for a moment as she took in the bustling market, the laughter and conversations washing over her like a wave of warmth. It was something she longed for but could never have within the House for Girls. Miss Skelton did not even like them to be near to the market, as though afraid they would smile too much for her liking.

Sighing, Elsbeth turned her back to the busy Smithfield Market and focused on her task, hoping she might be able to linger for a little while after she'd finished her task.

"Are you selling these?"

Jerked from her thoughts, Elsbeth turned to see a young man standing a short distance away from her, his eyes bright and a lazy smile on his face. Schooling her features into one of nothing more than general amiableness, she shook her head.

"No, I'm afraid not, sir. I am to place these around the railings." She did not say why, not wanting to encourage the young man to come to the Smithfield House for the ball, not when he clearly knew this was where she was from.

"I see." He moved closer to her, his smile still

lingering – and Elsbeth felt herself shrink back within herself. He was clearly something of a rake, for with his fine cut of clothes and his highly polished boots, there was no doubt that he was a gentleman – and gentlemen, from what she knew, often thought they could get whatever they wished.

He was still watching her intently, his dark brown eyes warm as they lingered on her. His dark hair was swept back, revealing his strong jaw. With his strong back and broad shoulders, Elsbeth was sure that he sent many young ladies hearts beating wildly with hopes of passion, but she had never felt more intimidated.

"Do excuse me," she murmured, making to turn away from him but only for him to catch her elbow.

"Do let me buy one from you," he said, his breath brushing across her cheek. "To remember you by, my fair flower."

Elsbeth felt a curl of fear in her stomach but chose to stand tall, her chin lifted. "No, I thank you, but I cannot sell one to you. I have a job to do. Do excuse me."

She wrenched her elbow from his hand and turned away again, telling herself to remain strong in the face of his oozing self-importance. She did not like him at all, despite his handsome features, for it was clear that he expected a simple compliment to overwhelm her to the point that she would do just as he wished.

"Well, if you will not sell one to me then perhaps you might converse with me for a time," the gentleman continued, his smile a little faded from his expression. "I am greatly inclined to know who you are."

Concentrating on tying a bunch of flowers to the railings, Elsbeth focused intently on her task so that she would not have to answer him immediately. She could see his smile disappearing altogether as he waited, his irritation mounting – and she felt the same sense of triumph as when she had set Miss Skelton to rights only yesterday.

"You need not concern yourself with someone as lowly as I," she replied eventually, barely giving him a glance. "I am sure you have more than a few beautiful young ladies in your acquaintance."

He chuckled, not taking her brush off with any kind of sincerity.

"I may very well do, miss, but they do not all intrigue me as you do."

Biting back a groan of frustration, Elsbeth tried to continue on with her task as quickly as she could, finding it more and more difficult to concentrate as the young man continued to follow her along the railing.

"Must I beg you for a flower?" he laughed, putting his hand over hers for a moment as she tried to tie the next bunch to the railings. "Come now, a name then, in exchange for your reluctance to give me a beautiful bloom."

A heat rose into her face as Elsbeth pulled her hand away, disliking this man more and more.

"I do not think that necessary," she replied, firmly, looking into his expectant face and hoping that, somehow, he would leave her be. "I will not be engaging in any kind of flirtation with you today, sir, so I would ask that you leave me to my task."

The mirthful look on his face began to die away, his lips flattening and eyes growing dull. Clearly, he was not in the least bit used to having such a straightforward refusal.

"Good day, sir," she said again, trying to build her courage by remaining exactly where she was and looking into his face without any kind of hesitation. "Now do excuse me."

Letting out a long breath of relief, Elsbeth watched out of the corner of her eye as the young gentleman stepped back, let out his breath in a huff and began to walk away from her, evidently very out of sorts from her rebuffing of his charms. She could not help but be glad that he had left her alone, hating the thought of even seeing him again. He unsettled her in a way that had left her almost stricken with fright, for she had been forced to battle her way through their conversation in an attempt to keep up her courage.

"A ball, you say?"

Horrified, Elsbeth's head shot up as she heard the young man's voice drift towards her, seeing him talking to an older gentleman who was indicating Smithfield House with his walking stick.

"And how might one procure an invitation?"

Elsbeth closed her eyes, tightly. She did not want this particular gentleman to attend, praying that Miss Skelton would not allow a late invitation but yet fully aware that this was exactly what she would do.

Her fingers slipped as she tried to continue tying the string around the bunch of flowers, her ears straining to hear what the young gentleman was saying. She was aware that he was still watching her, could feel his eyes on her as she hurried to finish, desperate to get back inside and away from his intimidating gaze.

"Then I simply *must* see what I can do to obtain such an invitation," she heard the young man say, loudly. "I am quite certain that I can convince whoever is in charge that I simply must be allowed to attend."

The older man he was talking to laughed aloud. "I do not think you need concern yourself in that, my dear Lord Radford! To have a viscount amongst them would be a wonderful event in itself!"

A viscount.

Her heart sank. Miss Skelton would grasp at the opportunity to have a viscount at their ball, which would mean that, unless Elsbeth could find a way to excuse herself from all the proceedings – which was highly doubtful – she would be forced to see the young man again.

Her stomach churned as Lord Radford made a show of walking through the iron gate towards the front of the large House, his eyes lingering on her and a broad, proud smile plastered across his face. She shook her head to herself and turned her whole body away from him, refusing to give him even the smallest bit of her attention any longer.

She heard a faint chuckle, the arrogance of him making her hands curl into fists. This man had no consideration for anyone other than himself, it seemed, believing that he was going to not only find out her name but also acquaint himself with her more fully.

"I will not allow myself to be married off to any man,"

she muttered to herself, tying the last bunch of blooms to the railings with a little more force than she had intended. "I will have my independence. I will have my freedom. And nothing that either Miss Skelton or an arrogant young gentleman presumes will make any difference."

CHAPTER THREE

The following evening found Elsbeth trying desperately to come up with some kind of excuse as to why she simply could not attend the Smithfield House ball, even though Miss Skelton had already ensured everything was in place.

"You have a new ballgown, Elsbeth. Your benefactor granted you a substantial amount of money for this so you must be careful with it."

Miss Skelton walked into Elsbeth's bedchamber without either knocking or introducing herself, just as she always did.

"Thank you, Miss Skelton," Elsbeth replied, through gritted teeth, wishing she could find something else to say that would express her discontent at both the lady's rudeness and her own disinclinations towards the ball.

"You have slippers also. I expect you to make a good impression on all the gentlemen who attend this evening," Miss Skelton continued, grandly. "Given your status in society, it is best that you attempt to open as many doors as possible, Elsbeth. That includes the possibility of a husband."

"I will not marry, Miss Skelton," Elsbeth retorted before she could stop herself. "I have no intention of doing so."

Miss Skelton's beady eyes landed on her with such a fierceness that Elsbeth was forced to catch her breath.

"You will do all you can, Elsbeth, for you know very well I want you gone from this house," Miss Skelton hissed, her grand and calm demeanor gone in an instant. "You are not wanted, you are not welcome. Do I make myself clear?"

Elsbeth got to her feet, her hands planted firmly on her hips. "This is my life, Miss Skelton, and I will do with it as I please. I will not be forced into matrimony; I will not be forced into anything I do not wish." She lifted her chin a notch and held Miss Skelton's gaze firmly. "I am well aware that you do not want my company nor my presence in Smithfield House but I will remain here for as long as I choose."

"With what funds?" Miss Skelton sneered, her eyes narrowing. "I have told you that your benefactor will withdraw his funding by the end of this year."

Having been about to retort that she knew very well this was not the case, Elsbeth bit her tongue hard and tasted blood. If she said anything like that, then Mrs. Banks would be the one in the firing line, and she could not allow that.

"Then I will remain here until the end of the year," she replied, calmly. "And we will see what my benefactor does then, shan't we? Perhaps he, whomever he is, will surprise us both." She lifted one eyebrow, looking towards Miss Skelton with a determined air and saw the woman's eyes narrow further.

It was clear she was somewhere between anger and suspicion, as though Elsbeth had surprised her by speaking so plainly. However, Elsbeth did not back down, continuing to keep her gaze pinned on Miss Skelton as she held her chin high and her hands on her hips. She was not about to allow Miss Skelton to continue to demand that she do whatever it was she asked, finding a new strength filling her. This was the start of her new life. A life where she did not have to agree, did not have to do, did not have to behave in a certain way at a certain time in a certain place. There would be no need for her to go to the ball this evening. She would not have to wear the gown nor dance with whichever cloying gentleman wished to take her hand in his.

"Whatever it is you are planning, Elsbeth, you had better watch that tongue of yours," Miss Skelton whispered, malevolently. "If you truly believe that you can continue on in this house with that kind of attitude, then I will tell you now that you are wrong. Whatever you think about yourself, you had best remember that it is still I who holds the power in this House."

"I will not be treated as though I have no right to my own life!" Elsbeth exclaimed, her anger bursting out in a torrent. "I am doing what I can to find a new position far away from here, but I will not be shoehorned into matrimony! You cannot insist upon that."

Miss Skelton's lip curled. "You really are a most disgraceful young lady, Elsbeth. I thought I had trained you better than that. Why Lord Radford has any interest in you, I simply cannot understand." She sneered at Elsbeth as she stepped forward, her whole expression telling Elsbeth that she was walking on very thin ice – and yet Elsbeth did not care.

"You will do exactly as you are told, else I shall withhold my references from your applications," she continued, as Elsbeth struggled to find a decent retort. "The dream of being a governess will disappear the moment I refuse to write you a reference."

Elsbeth was so angry that, for a long moment, she could not speak. She could feel heat searing her cheeks, feel fury coursing through her veins, setting her whole body alight, but still, she could not speak. She wanted to shout that this did not matter, that she would simply remain here until she was twenty-one if she had to, but she knew she could not.

"I will not be going to the ball this evening, Miss Skelton," she replied, her voice trembling as she struggled to keep her emotions in check. "I will not be attending in any way. Lord Radford will have to simply enjoy his own company for a time."

Miss Skelton did not move nor speak for a few minutes. There was no expression on her face as she looked back at Elsbeth, although her face was a little paler than before.

"You *will* attend, Elsbeth, else I shall send Mrs. Banks out from this establishment. Do you understand me? I will terminate her position here if you do not show at this ball. This is your choice, Elsbeth. Either you do as expected or Mrs. Banks will lose her place in the only house she has called home these last fifteen years." She gave a slight shrug and turned away from Elsbeth, walking back towards the door. "The choice is yours, Elsbeth."

Elsbeth went cold all over, realizing that Miss Skelton had her over a barrel. She knew full well that Elsbeth would do anything for Mrs. Banks, which meant that she *would* go to the ball this evening after all, *would* dance and converse with the gentlemen there and *would* listen to them when they spoke. That included the hateful Lord Radford, with his arrogant ways and determined smile. Sinking into her seat, Elsbeth let out a long groan and buried her face in her hands, feeling hot tears pricking at the corners of her eyes.

She had no choice. She had thought that, finally, she would be able to start making decisions about her own life, would be able to determine what it was she could do, but now, it seemed, Miss Skelton continued to hold the reins of her life. She was to be tossed about, from one place to the next, simply by Miss Skelton's demand.

Tears began to flow through her fingers as she wept, feeling both hurt and confused by Miss Skelton's hatred of her. Why she would go to such lengths as to threaten to hurt Mrs. Banks, just to force her to remain at the ball, to force her to consider gentlemen that she'd never met before in life?

You are not wanted.

Her tears still flowing, Elsbeth got up from the bed and looked at the smooth, unblemished silk of her new gown. It was beautiful, almost seeming to glow as she ran her fingers down it gently.

You are not welcome.

This was why Miss Skelton was doing all she could to force Elsbeth to attend the ball. She did not care whether or not Elsbeth became a governess, a seamstress or a wife, just so long as she left her establishment as soon as possible. Perhaps she knew that Elsbeth's chances of finding a suitable position as a governess were somewhat slim, given her status and her lack of proper parentage, so was determined to have her meet as many gentlemen as possible in the hope that one might take Elsbeth off her hands. On top of which, Lord Radford appeared to have spoken to her about his interest in Elsbeth, which made her almost sick to her stomach.

She wanted nothing to do with him and, whilst she knew she had no other choice but to attend this evening's festivities, it did not mean that she would have to accept any kind of invitation to further her acquaintance with anyone, including Lord Radford.

Wiping her eyes, Elsbeth tried not to let her feelings of panic rise up and overwhelm her, knowing that to do so would allow Miss Skelton to win a great victory. She would dress and go down to the ball as expected, but she would keep her head held high, her stance firm and her gaze determined. Miss Skelton would see that she was not withering underneath her threatening words, but would see her stand tall, doing what she had to because she loved Mrs. Banks like a mother. There was no shame in that.

. . .

It was, however, with great trepidation that Elsbeth made her way down the stairs and into the large hall that was used for dining each day, seeing it now transformed into a ballroom – although it was not particularly grand in any way. There were lanterns and candlesticks set up around the room, with a wide-open floor for the dancing. There was also a table at one end which held refreshments, and Elsbeth knew there would be a short break in the middle of the evening where a light supper would be served.

Her stomach was in knots as she descended carefully, hoping she did not draw too much attention. The gown she had on was the most beautiful thing she had ever worn, her long gloves matching the shade perfectly. One of the maids had surpassed herself with Elsbeth's hair, for it now seemed to curl beautifully whilst being kept piled up high on her head, with only a few tendrils escaping to whisper around her forehead. Her slippers were soft and warm and a single diamond glittered in a pendant that she wore around her neck – it was the only piece of jewelry she owned and, whilst she had always had it, she had never known where it came from. And, of course, Miss Skelton had never told her.

Miss Skelton was watching her, a grim smile on her face as Elsbeth descended into the ballroom. Elsbeth caught her eye but did not look away, determined not to be ashamed. She would not marry any of these gentlemen here tonight, even though she would have to converse and dance with them all. Miss Skelton was not to force her into matrimony, no matter how hard she tried.

"And finally, my flower, I have learned your name."

Elsbeth jerked to attention as she heard the familiar voice of Lord Radford in her ear, turning swiftly and, just a moment afterwards, stepping away from him.

"We do observe propriety here, my lord," she murmured, looking over his shoulder so that she would not have to see his arrogant features. "You are standing much too close."

He chuckled but did not move forward again, rubbing his hands together in a way that made Elsbeth shudder.

"Miss Skelton has informed me that you are Miss Elsbeth Blakely, my dear lady, and I am very glad to make your acquaintance. I am Viscount Andrew Radford."

He bowed and Elsbeth, despite her determination not to give him more than a single moment of her attention, curtsied as gracefully as she could, aware that Miss Skelton would be watching her.

"Now, where is your dance card?" Lord Radford exclaimed, his eyes roving over her figure towards her hands. "I must sign as many dances as I can."

She lifted her chin, her demeanor cool. "I am afraid, Lord Radford, that I do not wish to dance with you. Do excuse me."

Hearing his sharp intake of breath, Elsbeth winced inwardly, far too aware that he would go to Miss Skelton about her behavior towards him and prayed desperately that it was not a step too far. Mrs. Banks' position was at stake, but she simply could not bring herself to dance with the arrogant gentleman who looked at her as though she were nothing more than a delicious morsel he could not wait to pick clean.

"I beg your pardon, Miss Blakely?"

Closing her eyes for a moment, Elsbeth turned to see Lord Radford coming after her, his cheeks a mottled red.

"Yes, Lord Radford?"

"I procured an invitation to this evening so that I might dance with you and further our acquaintance," he spluttered, more than a little angry. "And you have the gall to turn me down?"

Elsbeth gave him a small, tight smile as the music began for the first dance. "Lord Radford, whatever gave you the impression that I was interested in furthering my acquaintance with you?"

His mouth fell open for a moment as he stared at her, only for him to shake his head in apparent disbelief.

"I believe I made my feelings quite clear when we spoke earlier today, Lord Radford," she continued when he said nothing. "I can tell that you are a gentleman used to being given all that you desire but I am afraid I will not be so inclined."

Lord Radford swallowed hard, his brows furrowing together and his jaw clenched. "Miss Blakely, I was led to understand that you require either a husband or a protector." He shrugged, his gaze drifting over her form. "I am not yet inclined to marry so a protector would suit me very well as it would you, I understand, since you are so determined to have a modicum of freedom."

Elsbeth felt herself go cold all over, her hands beginning to shake as she looked back at him, hardly believing what he had just said. Clenching her hands together in front of her, she drew in a long, steadying breath before speaking, knowing exactly where such a suggestion had come from.

"And might I ask, Lord Radford, if this supposed knowledge came from Miss Skelton?"

"It did," he replied, without even the slightest hesitation. "As she is in charge here, I thought it to be the truth."

"Then you are quite mistaken!" Elsbeth exclaimed as the music rose to a crescendo behind her. "I am not looking for a protector. I am to be a governess, or a teacher, depending on what situation I can find. I am not a poor and lowly lady who will fall into your arms and thrust my favors upon you so that you might pay me in return. How dare you think of me in such a way!"

Despite her anger, Elsbeth noticed that Lord Radford appeared to be rather disconcerted, his expression growing almost horrified as he looked back at her. Elsbeth had no doubt that Miss Skelton had been the one to tell him such a thing, using his interest in Elsbeth for her own ends, but what on earth had made Miss Skelton think that she would ever have accepted?

An icy hand gripped her heart as she studied Lord Radford, her breath slowly leaving her body.

"You thought to try and force me into such a situation," she breathed, stumbling back from him. "You were sent over to me in order to try and persuade me, one way or the other, to do your bidding, to become your mistress." She clapped one hand over her mouth, horrified and terror-stricken. "Get away from me."

"No, Miss Blakely, no, I never thought to do anything

of the sort," Lord Radford protested at once, his hand reaching for her. "I spoke to Miss Skelton and –"

"Your association with Miss Skelton tells me everything I need to know about your character, Lord Radford," Elsbeth interrupted, turning her back on him. "Now leave me be. I do not wish to exchange even another word with you for the rest of the evening."

CHAPTER FOUR

Viscount Andrew Radford was angry and humiliated. He had thought that the lady he had been pursuing would be more than willing to speak to him and to dance with him and certainly had not intended to make his proposal to her so soon, but her reaction to him had been both horrifying and shaming.

He did not understand it. When he had spoken to Miss Blakely earlier that day, she had seemed cold and disinterested, but he had put that down to the fact that he was speaking to her in a public place, where she had to be on her guard as regarded her behavior. She was, by all accounts, an orphan, or at the very least, someone whose parentage was unknown, which meant that society already looked down on her somewhat. And yet he had been captured by the beauty of her eyes, the windswept hair that tumbled out of its pins and down her shoulders. She appeared so free, so unhindered, that he had been drawn to her.

To discover that there was a ball for gentlemen such

as he to attend had been a pleasant surprise in itself, and to find Miss Skelton so willing to have his presence there had been wonderful. When he had mentioned the lady at the front of Smithfield House, he had been astonished at Miss Skelton's eagerness to speak of her. Within a few minutes, he knew her name, how long she had been at the House for Girls and that she had a dowry to her name that was rather substantial. He had quietly asked about the girl's benefactor, but Miss Skelton had shaken her head, saying she knew very little.

Not that the dowry mattered to him, being a viscount, for he had more than enough wealth. Nor did he intend to marry and had said so to Miss Skelton, whilst still mentioning his interest in the lady. As far as he knew, the ladies that lived in this House required an income that would keep them housed and fed for the rest of their lives, and he had to wonder whether or not that income had to come from proper means.

What he was hoping for had been quite improper.

Miss Skelton, however, had not seemed in the least bit put out by his careful mention of what he had to offer the lady, eagerly expressing how glad she was to hear of his inclinations and that she was quite sure Miss Blakely would be willing to listen to his proposal, if not to take on the role as soon as she could. This had surprised him, given that Miss Skelton was meant to care for the ladies who resided in the Smithfield House, but then Andrew had realized just how many young ladies passed through these doors and all had become clear in his mind. Miss Skelton required young ladies to find suitable situations very soon after they came of age, for the following year she would have even more young ladies to care for....and not all of them could become governesses now, could they? And even fewer would become wives.

However, now it appeared that Miss Blakely had no notion of becoming anyone's mistress, least of all his. He did not know whether to be angry with Miss Skelton for misleading him, or with himself for pursuing a young lady simply because she intrigued him. After all, this ball did not exactly match up to his usual social events. He was much more inclined to spend his time around high society, mixing with earls and viscounts instead of baronets and knights!

"I do apologize, Lord Radford, for how Miss Blakely spoke to you. Might I please ask you to forgive her outburst?"

Coming to a standstill, Andrew looked down at a small, rather round lady who was looking up at him with grave concern in her eyes.

"She did not mean to insult you, Lord Radford, I am sure," the lady continued, almost desperately. "I will speak to her myself, of course."

Andrew sighed. "And might I ask who you are?"

The lady colored, bobbing a curtsy. "Of course. Do excuse me. Mrs. Banks is my name and I teach the girls here at Smithfield House."

He lifted one eyebrow. "You teach them?"

"All manner of things," Mrs. Banks replied, as they began to walk together to the edge of the room. "Including the truth that they can choose their own path in life. Miss Blakely is determined not to marry as yet,

Lord Radford, although she should have made that clear to you in a less fraught manner."

He shook his head, another sigh tearing from his lips. "I did not ask her to marry me, Miss Banks, if that is your concern."

She blinked up at him, clearly confused.

"It was a rather *different* proposal, if you catch my meaning," he replied, not caring in the least what the lady thought of him. "Miss Blakely made her disinclination very clear."

Mrs. Banks frowned at once, her cheeks growing red as her eyes narrowed, spitting fire.

"How dare you?" she whispered, speaking to him as though he were her son and she his ever-proper mother. "This is not that kind of establishment and Miss Blakely certainly is not that kind of lady!"

"I was encouraged to do so!" he exclaimed, growing frustrated with the lady and, in fact, the entire situation. "It appears I have been misled."

The anger faded from Mrs. Banks expression almost at once, although the frown remained.

"Miss Skelton seemed to suggest that Miss Blakely would be more than willing to do as I asked, but it appears she was wrong," he continued, making to move past her. "Do excuse me."

"My lord."

He looked down to see Mrs. Banks' hand on his arm, which both surprised and irritated him. He was forced to remind himself that he was not at one of his usual balls and that, therefore, his expectations ought not to be in any way similar, but still, the fact that she had caught him in such a way was most improper.

"Miss Skelton does not care one jot for that girl, Lord Radford," Mrs. Banks said firmly, her jaw clenched. "I would not listen to a word she says about Miss Blakely, for she is determined to have her gone from this place in any way she can."

A twinge of interest tugged at Andrew's mind. "And why is that, Mrs. Banks? What is it about Miss Blakely that makes Miss Skelton treat her so?"

The lady shook her head, her hand dropping from his arm as she turned her head away. "I do not know, Lord Radford. Forgive me, I should not have spoken so openly with you, but I must know that Miss Blakely is being taken care of in the best way possible. I would advise you not to heed anything Miss Skelton has said about her for, as I said, her intentions towards her are not kind."

Andrew nodded slowly, seeing the pained expression on Mrs. Banks features and realizing that she did, in fact, truly care for the girls she taught.

"Thank you, Mrs. Banks," he murmured, inclining his head. "I will heed your advice."

"And you will not speak of Miss Blakely's behavior to Miss Skelton?" Mrs. Banks asked anxiously, as he made to turn away. "I am fearful of what she would do, Lord Radford."

He nodded again. "Of course I will not," he replied smoothly. "Good evening, Mrs. Banks."

Moving away from her, Andrew found himself filled with a sudden curiosity over the beautiful Miss Blakely. If what Mrs. Banks said was true, then there was some reason that Miss Skelton disliked the lady, although he could not guess why. She intrigued him even more than before, despite her robust refusal to engage with him in any way.

"You are being ridiculous, Radford," he muttered to himself, as he wandered to the table of refreshments and picked up a glass of something that appeared to be champagne. "Forget about her and find someone else to consider."

Turning around, Andrew took in the many young ladies that were dotted about the floor, seeing them smile and laugh with the gentlemen that had joined them. None of them caught his interest in the way Miss Blakely had. In fact, Andrew found himself searching for her, his eyes moving past the other ladies within a few seconds.

"My dear Lord Radford, I do hope you have had a chance to speak to Miss Blakely," said a familiar voice as Miss Skelton came to stand by him. "I saw her speaking with you. I do hope everything is quite all right."

He cleared his throat and saw the worried eyes of Mrs. Banks watching him closely from across the room. "Of course, Miss Skelton. Why would there be any difficulty?"

Miss Skelton said nothing but gave a slight shrug, her eyes watching him with such intensity that for a moment, Andrew wondered if she was able to read his thoughts and see exactly what it was he was thinking.

"I assure you, Miss Skelton, Miss Blakely was nothing but amiable towards me, and I did find myself enjoying our rather spirited discussion."

"I see," Miss Skelton murmured, sounding somewhat disbelieving. "And are you to dance with her later?"

Andrew felt his mouth go dry as he struggled to think of an answer. Mrs. Banks was still staring at him from across the room, but he still could not think of a reasonable explanation as to why he did not have his name on her dance card.

"I believe Miss Blakely is looking to be a governess or a teacher," he stammered, changing the subject completely. "She did not accept my request as to her possible.... position with me and as such, I did not feel it right to request a dance from her. I do hope you understand, Miss Skelton."

As he looked at the older woman, he saw her brows almost meet as she frowned, her lips pressing together in fury – and Andrew felt himself quail even though her anger was not to be directed towards himself. He realized now why Mrs. Banks appeared so afraid of what Miss Skelton would say, finding his usually selfish heart growing somewhat concerned for Miss Blakely.

"I would not, of course, lay any blame at Miss Blakely's feet," he continued, hastily. "The truth is, Miss Skelton, I was considering whether or not I might offer her a position."

The words fell from his lips without any true consideration, but now that they had been said aloud, he could not take them back. Miss Skelton narrowed her eyes all the more.

"Miss Blakely should accept whatever position she can get, Lord Radford," she said, crisply, her eyes looking over his shoulder in the hopes of spotting the girl. "If you have offered her a position under your protection, then I am saddened that she has not accepted it. However, if you were to offer her such a role in your house as governess, then perhaps you might be able to get what you wish from her regardless."

Andrew tried not to let his mouth fall open, aware of what Miss Skelton was suggesting.

"After all, I am certain that most gentlemen make sport of their governesses or even their maids, do they not?" Miss Skelton continued, crisply. "I shall inform Miss Blakely that she is to be your new governess. What children do you have, Lord Radford?"

Not quite certain how he had managed to ensure Miss Blakely's presence in his home, Andrew cleared his throat. "My niece is due to arrive next week and will be staying for the summer. Her parents – my brother and his wife – are away on business and have requested that the girl stay with me." He rolled his eyes, sighing heavily. "*Why* they cannot leave her at home with a governess and nursemaid there, I cannot understand, but they insist on bringing her to me."

The truth was that, whilst the child was to remain at his house, Andrew had no intention of taking any kind of interest in the girl, for she was already being cared for by her nurse. There was not a governess to speak of as yet, but at four years of age, he was certain that the child could do with one. What he did not mention to Miss Skelton was his other child who remained back in his own country estate, hidden from society for the time being. She had her own nurse to care for her, as well as most of his staff wrapped around her little finger even though she was but four years old. Whilst she would, in time, require a governess, he did not think that it would take him too long to convince Miss Blakely to do as he asked and become his mistress instead of a governess. In that regard, the presence of his niece in his home for a couple of months would do very well. He would simply find his charge another governess when the time came, so that he could continue enjoying the delight that was Miss Blakely.

"I see," Miss Skelton replied, sounding somewhat disinterested. "Then next week, I shall have Miss Blakely at your door, ready to take on her duties. You will pay her, I presume?"

"Of course," Andrew stammered, still a trifle confused. "But, with all due respect, Miss Skelton, I have not yet asked Miss Blakely if she would be willing to take on this role and neither have you. What if she is to refuse?"

Miss Skelton appeared to smile, her lips stretching over her thin face as her eyes glittered malevolently. "You need not worry in that regard, Lord Radford. I am sure Miss Blakely will be more than willing. In fact, I give you my promise that Miss Blakely will agree to your request and will be at your door a week from today."

Andrew frowned, still feeling as though something was a little wrong with this entire situation and worried that he was, somehow, putting Miss Blakely into an untenable situation. But then he recalled her beauty, the way she intrigued him so, and he decided to go along with all that Miss Skelton said, regardless of his concerns. To have Miss Blakely in his home as a governess, even if only for a couple of months, would mean that there was the chance he might be able to encourage her into his bed, which would then lead to her becoming his mistress. He could make it so that she had her own home, her own staff and was content in everything, so long as she continued to accept his affections. Perhaps all it would take was time.

"Thank you, Miss Skelton. I look forward to having Miss Blakely as part of my household," he said, with a broad smile, pushing away his concerns and niggling anxiety. "You will make all the arrangements, I trust?"

Her smile broadened. "But of course, Lord Radford." She gave him a small bow, instead of curtsying, which Andrew returned. "Do excuse me. I must speak to some other gentlemen in the hope of making similar arrangements for the rest of my girls."

He nodded. "Of course, I quite understand. Thank you again."

As Miss Skelton walked away, Andrew tried not to let the smile fade from his features as he thought about Miss Blakely and her supposed willingness to be part of his household staff. The way Miss Skelton had spoken, she had made it sound as though Miss Blakely would agree to it regardless of her own personal feelings, although he could not imagine the spitfire that was Miss Blakely to be so easily swayed.

But, then again, perhaps that was no concern of his. He would get what he wanted and that was enough to satisfy him. In time, he was sure he could convince Miss Blakely to do as he wished. A short stay in his home as governess would prove that to her.

A small, satisfied smile spread across his face as he tossed his concerns aside, refusing to consider them any longer. Miss Blakely would be in his house by the end of the following week and, in time, Andrew was sure he would get what he wanted from her.

All he had to do was wait.

CHAPTER FIVE

Her face burning crimson, Elsbeth stepped into Lord Radford's drawing room, her hands clasped in front of her as she lifted her chin and stared at the man responsible for her sudden change in circumstances.

Lord Radford rose from his chair at once, a delighted smile on his face as he walked towards her, but Elsbeth did not return it. She did not want to be here. She did not want to so much as speak to this gentleman but, for her, there had been no other choice.

"Ah, Miss Blakely," Lord Radford exclaimed, looking her up and down. "May I say just how very professional you look. Quite different from last week's ball, I must say!"

Elsbeth bit back her harsh retort, closing her eyes for a moment as she felt Lord Radford's gaze rake her up and down.

"A governess, eh?" Lord Radford chuckled, as she

opened her eyes. "Very good, Miss Blakely, very good. Come over here and sit down so that I can discuss your duties."

Stiffly, Elsbeth followed him towards a seat by the fire, which was warming the whole room on what was a rather cold summer's day. She perched on the edge of the chair, hating that she had been forced into this position instead of being allowed to consider her own future.

And she knew exactly who to blame.

"Miss Skelton made all the arrangements, then, just as she said," Lord Radford murmured, as a maid came in with the tea tray. "Now, Miss Blakely, if you would not mind pouring for us both."

She looked at him, one eyebrow raised. "Lord Radford, I am not here as your companion."

He looked back at her steadily. "Pour the tea, Miss Blakely."

Sitting back in her chair, Elsbeth folded her arms and looked back at him steadily. She'd known from the very first moment that Miss Skelton had spoken to her of Lord Radford that the man had more to his intentions than merely employing her as a governess. She could still hear herself shouting at Miss Skelton that she would rather die than work for that man, only for Miss Skelton to slap her, hard, across the face and demand she do so, else Mrs. Banks would be on the line.

It was the only soft spot that Elsbeth had and, now that Miss Skelton had found it, she had chosen to use it to her advantage. Elsbeth had been forced to come here, forced to do what she did not want to do, all because she loved Mrs. Banks too much to see her come to harm. The thought of the lady out on the street, with no home to go to and no family to turn to for help had been too much and so, Elsbeth had been given no other choice but to capitulate.

However, she was not about to allow Lord Radford to treat her as though she were a friend, a companion, a.... a mistress. She knew precisely that this was what he wanted from her, although guessed that he would never force the matter which was why he'd come up with the idea of her playing governess for a time.

It does not matter what he wants, she told herself, as she kept her gaze steady. *You are strong. Do not give in now.*

If she was to lean forward, pour the tea and do as he asked, then Lord Radford could very easily be led to believe that she was a weak-willed young lady, willing to do whatever he asked now that she had been forced into this position. However, she would not allow herself to be so treated. She would not pour the tea. She would take on her role as a governess with all seriousness, refusing to be treated as anything less than or as anything more than that.

"Good gracious, you are somewhat stubborn, are you not? Lord Radford chuckled, with no irritation in his words. "What is it, Miss Blakely? You do not wish to pour the tea?"

"I am not here as your guest, Lord Radford. I am your governess and, as such, do not require such things as this. This is to be a formal meeting, I presume, where you might lay out my role for me so that I might begin this very day."

Lord Radford shook his head and chuckled again, reaching for the teapot so that he might pour the tea for them both.

"There, you see," he grinned, handing her a cup which she had no choice but to take. "You need not be so stiff, Miss Blakely. This is a formal meeting, yes, but we can still drink tea and discuss your role, can we not?"

Elsbeth said nothing but sipped her tea carefully, finding the brew refreshing and yet feeling more and more uncomfortable with every second that passed. Lord Radford was handsome and being more than a little amiable, but she knew he was nothing more than a rake and a scoundrel, used to getting exactly what he wanted and doing whatever he could in order to achieve his aims. Just as he had done with her.

"You do not seem pleased to be in my home, Miss Blakely," Lord Radford murmured, looking at her thoughtfully. "I thought such a position was what you wanted."

A harsh laugh escaped her lips, seeming to surprise Lord Radford as much as it did her.

"Lord Radford, whilst you are correct in saying that I hoped for such a position as this, I also hoped that it would be of my own choosing." She hoped that he understood exactly what she meant and could see how she felt about it but, to her surprise, he merely shrugged.

"Well, things are as they are now, and I expect you to fulfill your role here as a governess. Some evenings, I will require your company."

Her eyes met his, disbelievingly. "My company?"

He shrugged again. "Yes. Precisely."

A lump formed in Elsbeth's throat as she saw the arrogance flash into Lord Radford's eyes again, seeing the way he simply expected her to do as he asked.

"Lord Radford, I am here as your governess to whichever child it is that lives with you and nothing more. I will not be anything more to you."

"Then I will let you go from my employ."

A spark of hope shot to her heart. "Please feel free to do so, Lord Radford. I have other options which I can pursue, most of which, I am sure, will be greatly more tenable than the situation here." Her words were forceful and sharp, her gaze direct and stance firm. She was not about to let Lord Radford dictate to her in the same way as Miss Skelton had. Whilst she could not return to Smithfield House, she would do whatever she had to until she was twenty-one. Whether that meant living on the streets of London, begging for food, or even taking up position as a scullery maid, she would do what was necessary. Anything except becoming Lord Radford's mistress.

He looked back at her gravely, his brow furrowing but Elsbeth did not back down. Lord Radford, despite being a viscount, had to understand that she was not about to do as he wished simply because of his title and fortune. She was more than that, whether he could see it in her or not.

"You are something of a challenge, I grant you, Miss Blakely," he murmured, after a few torturous minutes. "It appears my threats do not have any effect on you."

Swallowing hard, Elsbeth drank her tea carefully,

trying to show a relaxed and calm demeanor even though, inwardly, she was fighting tooth and nail to maintain control.

"You know what I want from you, Miss Blakely," he continued, bluntly. "And yet you continue to refuse. I am not inclined to force any woman into a situation she does not want to be in, but I confess that I find you intriguing and that, as yet, my interest has not diminished. You will remain here in my house as my niece's governess and, when I request it, you will come and converse with me. That is all I require."

Elsbeth wanted to refuse, wanted to shake her head and demand that he allow her to be entirely absent from his presence, but she was too weary to do so. This was, in fact, the best outcome she could have hoped for, given that she was now no longer expected to be in Lord Radford's company of an evening, knowing full well what that meant.

"We will only talk?"

Lord Radford's face split into a wide smile and, despite herself, Elsbeth grew aware of just how handsome a gentleman he truly was. His hazel eyes were warm and bright, his lopsided grin meant to charm her.

"Yes, Miss Blakely, we will only converse. That is, of course, unless you decide that you wish to accept my other offer of coming under my protection." He gave her a small shrug. "I can hope that, in time, you might choose to agree."

Her rage began to bubble again within her but, with sheer force of will, Elsbeth kept her expression calm. "I can assure you, Lord Radford, that will never be the case. I have my own life to live and I will not spend it doing another's bidding. I have spent too many years of my life doing just that and I know precisely how it feels to be so boxed in."

The smile faded from his expression, a note of interest in his voice. "Is that so, Miss Blakely? Well, well. It seems you have everything planned out. What if something entirely unexpected was to occur? Something that would throw you off your planned path?"

She rose to her feet, growing tired of him and his conversation. She was not about to start answering his questions and engaging in discussion with him about her private thoughts, hopes and dreams. This position, were she to actually be able to manage it for a prolonged length of time, was only serving to push her towards her goal. In a few years, she would be completely free.

"I would like to meet my charge, if I may, Lord Radford," she said, walking towards the door. "I would presume her to be in the nursery?"

His eyes fluttered over her again, despite the fact that she was clad in a long grey gown that had a high collar and long sleeves, hiding her curves completely. "I expect so," he replied, with a small shrug.

"Do you not wish to introduce me to her?"

It did not come as a surprise to Elsbeth that he shook his head, showing no interest in the child whatsoever.

"She will take to you very well, I am sure, Miss Blakely. The nurse will do the introductions if they are required. Now, this evening, I –"

"I will be very tired this evening, Lord Radford," Elsbeth interrupted, highly aware that she was speaking to him as though she was his equal but finding that this was the only way she was able to deal with his almost constant demands for her attentions. "Good day, my lord."

Before he could say anything more, before he could insist that she join him later that night, Elsbeth had pulled open the door and strode through it, closing it tightly behind her – much to the surprise of the butler. She did not stop but made her way back to her own room, which was located on the third floor of the townhouse. It was not particularly difficult to find, given that the house was not overly large. Her heart was thumping painfully as she climbed the stairs, suddenly feeling a strong urge to burst into tears. Drawing in long, steadying breaths, Elsbeth managed to make her way to her room without breaking her composure but, the moment the door closed behind her, she sank to the floor and began to cry.

Drawing her knees up, Elsbeth gave into the tears that had been threatening ever since Miss Skelton had informed her about her change in circumstances. She had not dared show even the slightest bit of emotion in front of Miss Skelton, determined not to break in front of her, but she had felt herself shatter inwardly. Having to say goodbye to Mrs. Banks had been the hardest of all, although, at least, Miss Skelton had allowed her some privacy in that regard.

Mrs. Banks had been all concern, not understanding why Elsbeth had chosen to go to Lord Radford's home, but Elsbeth had chosen not to tell her the truth, even though it had taken all of her strength not to utter a single word about Miss Skelton.

"You don't want to do this, do you?" Mrs. Banks had said, holding Elsbeth close. "I don't know what's going on, Elsbeth, but I can tell that something is very wrong about this."

How much she'd wanted to tell Mrs. Banks everything, how much she'd wanted to bare her soul as though, somehow, Mrs. Banks would be able to make everything all right! Instead, she'd kept her lips tightly shut, knowing that to say a single word about the matter would cause more problems. Mrs. Banks would either carry the guilt that was not hers to take over Elsbeth's new situation, or she would demand to speak to Miss Skelton and, in the process, most likely lose her position. It was not a risk Elsbeth had been able to take.

Her tears soaked into her governess' gown, making large dark patches on the already dull material. She hated this feeling of helplessness, of feeling as though she could not do anything to save herself. Whilst she knew that she could leave Lord Radford's home of her own free will, Elsbeth knew that she had nothing else waiting for her. Living her life on the streets of London did not bode well for a young lady such as she, even though she had told herself she would do it if she had no other choice. If Lord Radford made to put a hand on her, she would gather her things and leave his household at once, determined not to become the gentleman's plaything no matter how much he offered her. She would risk the streets of London if she had to.

"I am not that kind of lady," she said aloud, her voice

muffled by the heavy material of her dress as she rested her head on her knees. She thought she was so strong. She felt braver than she'd ever done before as she took a hold of her life, only for Miss Skelton to reveal that she was not in control of anything.

How much Miss Skelton must have hated her! Elsbeth still did not know the reason why the lady would push her into this situation, knowing full well of Lord Radford's true intentions, but she knew it came from a place of sheer hatred for Elsbeth. And, through using Lord Radford, Miss Skelton had achieved what she'd always longed for – Elsbeth to be gone from the Smithfield House for Girls.

Wiping her eyes carefully, Elsbeth looked around the small room she was now to call home. It had one large window which overlooked the streets of London, and on the other side sat a small fireplace with no fire in it currently, even though the room had a rather icy chill due to the lack of sunshine for the last couple of days. Her bed was in the corner, much similar to the one she had slept on in Smithfield House, and there was a small wardrobe for her things. The maid had already unpacked for her and, as Elsbeth looked, she saw that her hairbrush, pins and ribbons were set out on the small dressing table close to the window. She shook her head at the sight, knowing full well she did not require any kind of ribbons any longer. That was not appropriate for a governess and she certainly had no intention of wearing any kind of frippery when speaking to Lord Radford.

Her heart climbed into her throat as she thought of his demand that they meet sometimes in the evenings to talk. There was nothing she wanted to say to him and she certainly did not want to reveal anything about herself to the gentleman. He could talk as much as he wished and, whilst Elsbeth knew she would have to listen, it did not mean that she would have to engage with him. Lord Radford, she was sure, would talk a great deal about himself since that seemed to be the only person he cared about. He might hope that, in time, she would come around to his charms and allow herself to be put into a compromising position, but what Lord Radford did not seem to grasp was that the more he talked, the more he smiled, the less inclined she was towards him.

Yes, he was handsome, but it was his lack of character that pushed her away. She did not care for simply an attractive face, but rather found his selfish nature left him severely lacking. Perhaps, then, in time, he would see that his desire to converse with her, to urge her into the situation he wished for her to be in, was not about to be fulfilled.

Elsbeth imagined Lord Radford was not used to that.

Getting to her feet, Elsbeth dried her eyes as best she could and straightened her gown. She had to just get on with her new life, had to simply move forward and count each passing day as one step closer to her freedom. There was no use in her being upset or fraught over the situation, for it was not easily going to change. She would teach this niece of Lord Radford's and pray fervently every day that Lord Radford would simply leave her be.

Splashing some cold water on her face, Elsbeth dried her eyes and looked at her reflection in the small mirror, seeing her skin red and blotchy from where she had been crying. Her hair was, at least, still perfect in its tight bun and she had no pronounced wrinkles in her gown. Holding her head high, she made her way to the door and opened it, finding the corridor empty. Walking along the hallway, she soon found the nursery and, with a sharp knock, stepped inside.

CHAPTER SIX

Andrew took a long draw of his cigar, puffing out the smoke carefully as he let his eyes rove over the many books in his library – none of which he had read, of course. He did not care for reading in particular, finding it a rather dull pastime.

"Can I get you anything else, my lord?" the butler asked, setting down the small tray in front of him. "Should I alert the footmen as to your expected time of return to the house?"

"I do not think I intend to go out this evening, George," Andrew murmured, aware at the surprised expression on the butler's face, which was quickly hidden away. "You may retire, if you wish. As may the rest of the staff."

The butler hesitated for a moment before inclining his head. "Thank you, my lord."

Andrew chuckled to himself as the butler left the room, closing the door firmly behind him. He was well aware that this sudden desire to remain at home, behind closed doors, had taken the staff by surprise, but he felt no eagerness to go to Whites this particular evening. Perhaps it was due to the fact that his new governess had arrived only yesterday, and that his thoughts had been entirely caught up with her.

His brow caught with a frown. That in itself was rather unusual, was it not? Why was he so eager for Miss Blakely when he knew that he could have any other lady of his acquaintance? He only had to say the word and arms would be around his neck, kisses gently pressed to his lips, willing words whispered in his ear.

Taking another draw of his cigar, Andrew tried to come up with an answer to his own question, finding it difficult to explain what it was about Miss Blakely that tempted him so. She was beautiful in her own way, although he longed to see her hair flowing around her shoulders and her sky-blue eyes filled with something other than anger.

Perhaps it was because she simply presented him with a challenge he had not faced before. He had never been turned away by any lady to whom he had made his intentions more than obvious, regardless of their status in society and yet here came Miss Blakely with her outright refusal and her clear disdain. Mayhap he wanted to find a way to urge her into submission, to show her that she had nothing to fear from him. Perhaps he simply wanted to prove to her that the life he was offering her was a good life, one where she could be as free as she wished, so long as she kept her arms open towards him. Whatever it was, Andrew could not get free of her.

The door to the library suddenly flew open and, startled, Andrew saw Miss Blakely framed in the doorway, her face hidden in shadow.

"Miss Blakely!" he exclaimed, sitting up in his chair. "So, you came to speak to me after all! How fortuitous. I was just thinking that –"

"Your niece is only here for a short time?" she shouted, striding towards him as the door slammed shut behind her. "For a few months? That is how long I am to stay here for?"

He swallowed, hard.

"What is it you believe, Lord Radford? Do you believe that I will continue to remain in your house in *another* role by the time your niece is to return to her parents?"

That was exactly what he had hoped, although he could not exactly say as much to Miss Blakely, given how upset she appeared to be.

"No, of course not," he replied soothingly. "There is, of course, another explanation."

He saw the anger fade slightly from her eyes as she looked back at him, her hands slowly uncurling from their tight fists. However, he began to feel a little on edge, realizing that he had not thought this part of his plan through. He had believed that Miss Blakely would simply come around to his way of thinking in time but had never thought what her reaction might be to discover that the girl she was to teach was only with him for a month or two.

"Please, sit," he said, gesturing for her to sit down

opposite him. "I will not come near you, I promise, in case you are fearful that I might."

She glared at him but eventually did as he asked.

"Can I fetch you something to eat or drink?" he said, waving his hand towards the bell. "The butler will still be hard at work, I am sure."

"No."

Her voice was sharp and hard, slicing through him and making him wince inwardly. It was clear she did not want anything other than an explanation from him, her hands clasped tightly in her lap. Andrew watched her for a moment, his cigar smoking gently in his hand. Her face was pale, her hair falling out of her tight bun in wisps – but it was the look in her eyes that had him pause. It was clear she had been crying, for her eyes were puffy and red.

Guilt streaked through him like a flash of lightning. It was an uncomfortable sensation, given that he did not often feel guilty over anything he chose to do, and he found himself suddenly unable to look into her face.

"Lord Radford," she said, crisply, her voice shaking only a little. "What is it you intend for me to do here? Teach your niece for a month or so, only to have her return to her parents? She is so young that she is not quite ready for a governess, even though I do find her a very bright young lady."

His eyes darted to hers. "What is it you are saying, Miss Blakely?"

She drew in a long breath. "I will speak plainly, Lord Radford. You wish me to be in your bed, that much is apparent. However, I have continued to rebuff your advances and still, despite that, you have found a way to have me placed in your home against my better judgment. You have manipulated me and the course of my life simply to get what you want."

Looking away from her, Andrew felt heat rush up his spine and into his face, feeling as though he were some errant schoolboy in Eton being given a severe dressing down, yet knowing that he somehow deserved it.

"You have not considered anyone but yourself, Lord Radford," she continued, her voice shaking heavily with emotion. "I have been forced here only to find that your intentions for me are just the same as they once were, although you somehow believe that you will be able to convince me to give up my reputation, my standards, my very self simply to satisfy your whims. You will not take my refusal as my only answer, believing that, since you are used to always getting what you want, you will be able to achieve your aims with me. I am simply a toy for you to play with, something that you will have for a time until you grow bored and choose to discard me in whatever way you wish." She shook her head, her eyes glazing over with tears. "I will not allow myself to be treated so by anyone, Lord Radford, not even you with your high title, your wealth and status in society. I may be lesser than you in many ways but it does not mean that I should be treated with any less dignity and respect."

Her words came to a close, echoing around the room before settling themselves neatly into Andrew's heart. He could feel nothing but guilt and shame, her words sticking like needles into every part of him. This was not something he had ever experienced before and, to his horror, he felt his head lowering as the weight of her words settled on him like a heavy burden.

"You are quite right, Miss Blakely," he mumbled, not able to so much as lift his head. "You are quite right."

There was nothing but silence for a long time, whilst Andrew battled to keep his emotions from overwhelming him. Everything Miss Blakely had said was correct. He had not treated her with the respect she deserved, choosing to look at her as though she were nothing more than an object he could use for his own gratification. Did he truly believe that a lady was not to be treated with dignity simply because of her standing within society? Was that truly the kind of man he was?

A small groan escaped him as he sat forward, throwing his cigar into the fire before putting his head in his hands. In one moment, Miss Blakely had managed to pierce his heart and mind in a way no one had ever been able to do before. Suddenly, he was questioning everything, struggling to make sense of all that was going on in his heart.

"My goodness, I am nothing but a scoundrel."

He closed his eyes, recalling how his mother, the Dowager Radford, had so often pleaded with him to take the responsibilities of his title seriously, almost begging him to marry and produce an heir, as was expected. He had always brushed her off, laughing, telling her that he was enjoying life far too much to allow such a thing as family responsibility to hold him back. Besides, he'd always told himself that his brother had already married and had produced a child, albeit a girl, which meant that, most likely, there would soon be a son and a possible heir should the worst ever happen to him.

His world was spinning and it felt as though he was about to lose his grip at any moment. His breath was coming hard and fast, pain shooting through him as he squeezed his eyes shut. What kind of man was he?

You have manipulated me simply to get what you want.

"Miss Blakely, I – I must ask you to leave me," he said, hoarsely. "I do apologize. We can speak again tomorrow."

There was a short, tense, silence. "Lord Radford, you do not need to play games with me," came Miss Blakely's reply. "I am not inclined to give in easily to such theatrics."

He lifted his gaze to her, growing angry with her for disbelieving him only to realize that she had every right to do so. He had not given her any reason to trust him thus far and, therefore, he could easily understand why she had said such a thing.

"Miss Blakely, I can assure you that these are no theatrics," he replied, managing to sit up to look at her more carefully. "You have spoken to me in a way that no one else has ever dared to do." He shook his head, feeling as if his very soul had been broken open, spilling its blackness and darkness for all to see. "I am struggling to think clearly after what you have laid on my shoulders."

Miss Blakely's eyes narrowed.

"I have treated you repugnantly," he said heavily. "I have asked you to be something to me that you have every right to refuse. I should never have spoken to Miss Skelton about you."

She closed her eyes and, to his horror, Andrew saw a tear slipping down her cheek. Agony tore at his heart.

"Miss Skelton has always wanted me gone from her House for Girls," Miss Blakely replied, quietly, not opening her eyes. "It appears you gave her a wonderful opportunity to do just that."

His apology crumbled to dust in front of him. "I did not know." The memory of Mrs. Banks speaking to him shot to the forefront of his mind, torturing him again and forcing him to take back what he had just said. "I mean, I did hear something from Mrs. Banks but I was so completely wrapped up in what I wanted that I chose to speak to Miss Skelton regardless."

Opening her eyes, Miss Blakely looked back at him steadily, even though her eyes were swimming with tears. "Miss Skelton pushed me here in the knowledge that I would be gone from her House within a few short days, Lord Radford. She has long wanted me to be gone from her company and so, it seems, you were an answer to her prayers. And she to yours."

He wanted to refute that, wanted to say that it was not the case and that he had not meant to force her to come to his home, but his shame would not let him. Everything she had said was quite true.

"I had so many hopes," she continued, her voice breaking with emotion. "I hoped to have my freedom, to choose my own situation and then, in a few short years, be able to live the life I have always dreamed of, but instead, I was forced to come here at your bidding. The only thing I can do is continue to assure you that I will not be the person you wish me to be, Lord Radford. I will endure here because I have very little else open to me, but I swear to you here and now, that I will never willingly become your mistress."

Lowering his gaze, Andrew felt sweat bead on his brow.

"I quite understand, Miss Blakely. I will not press you on this any longer although I understand that you will not willingly believe me on this."

"No, Lord Radford, I will not," came the calm reply. "You cannot expect me to believe in such a sudden change of heart over the course of a single conversation."

"Then I shall prove it to you," he replied, thickly, suddenly desperate for her to leave so that he might wallow in his pain and embarrassment alone. These thoughts were tumultuous; pain bursting through his head as he tried to calm his whirling emotions. It was all becoming too much. "Miss Blakely, I have need of a governess back at my estate. I will not go into detail now but there you have it. Once your time here with my niece is over, I shall send you to my country estate to take on your duties there."

Managing to glance at her, he saw her expression to be one of confusion and doubt.

"It is not something that my staff here know of, however," he continued, both horrified and astonished that he had spoken of his charge with Miss Blakely. "Please keep the matter to yourself."

Miss Blakely shook her head, a small laugh of derision escaping her. "I hardly think so, Lord Radford. This is another scheme to –"

"No!" he exclaimed, slashing the air with his hand. "No, it is not, Miss Blakely. I am trusting you with information that I have fought to keep quiet for a very long time. You shall go alone to my country estate if you wish, to see for yourself." He shook his head before burying his hands into his hair, staring at the floor. "I shall speak to you again on all this in a few days' time, Miss Blakely. For the moment, I would like to be alone. I'm afraid your frankness has quite ended me."

He did not look at her again, too afraid to see what would be there when she rose from her seat. Waiting for her to close the door, he drew in long breaths, trying to steady the trembling that had begun to work all through him. Finally, the door closed tightly and he was left alone, his hands gripping on to his hair tightly as he tried to come to terms with what Miss Blakely had said to him.

He had been right to tell her that no one had ever spoken to him in such a way before. His friends were always eager to hear whatever stories he had to tell about his recent conquests, were always urging him on and, without hesitation, condoning his behavior. After all, it was simply what gentlemen did, was it not?

And still, he felt the heavy weight of shame settling on his shoulders.

Miss Blakely had been more open with him than anyone before. She'd told him exactly what she thought of his character, exactly what she saw of his nature, and Andrew had found he could not disagree. There was nothing for him *to* disagree with since it was all quite correct.

He was a cruel, selfish, arrogant gentleman and it had never bothered him until the moment Miss Blakely had stepped into his life. Suddenly, he found himself questioning everything he was, everything he thought he enjoyed, everything he thought he lived for, seeing himself in a whole new light. A light that revealed every drop of dirt on his skin, every bit of grime that had seeped into his soul.

And now, for whatever reason, he had told her about his charge back at the Radford Estate. He could not renege on his promise now, not when he was trying to prove to her that he would no longer pressure her to come to his bed as his mistress.

Letting out another loud groan, Andrew threw himself out of his chair and hurried towards the decanter, pouring himself a large glass of brandy which he swallowed in five large gulps. Pouring another – a smaller one this time – he made his way back towards the fire and looked into it, feeling the heat flicker across his face.

There was no thought of going to his bedchamber. He had too much to ponder, too much to consider, before his mind would let him rest. The shame he felt was agony, burning into his skin and branding him a rogue, a rascal, a scoundrel, a rake. He was not respectable or worthy of honor, and yet it was given to him regardless simply because of his title and status. Over the course of his life, he had simply come to expect such things, having never once considered how he treated those around him.

Setting his glass down on the mantlepiece, Andrew

squeezed his eyes closed as his head began to thump painfully. He would not sleep tonight, not when there was so much to consider. One thing was for certain, however. He would emerge in the morning a different man than the one who stood here now and perhaps, despite the pain, that would turn out to be a good thing.

CHAPTER SEVEN

One week later and still Lord Radford had not sent for her. In fact, Elsbeth had barely seen him. He was not often at home, although she had heard the footmen comment that the master had not gone to his usual haunts either – not that she knew what they were.

She thought back to that night as she tidied away the slate and the chalk from Miss Sarah's lesson, which had gone rather more smoothly than she had thought it would. Lord Radford had appeared to be tormented by what she'd said, but she had no idea how many of his words had been genuine. That being said, he had not appeared at her door or demanded that they meet to converse in order to try and convince her to give up her life as a governess. In fact, even though he had promised to speak to her again, he had not sent for her in the last week.

Elsbeth hated how much she thought of Lord Radford, even though she told herself it was simply because she wished to see whether or not Lord Radford had been honest in what he'd said. She still could not get the picture of him sitting with his head in his hands out of her mind. At one point, when he had dragged his gaze to hers, she had been sure that there had been tears in his eyes, but she had dismissed that thought almost at once, quite certain that he had been playing with her emotions.

But now, as the days had passed, she had become less and less certain of such a thing.

"That Miss Sarah's having her luncheon."

Turning around, Elsbeth smiled at the nurse, Mrs. Simpson, who had come back into the schoolroom to help Elsbeth tidy up. "I thought she did very well today."

"Yes, she did," Elsbeth agreed, thinking how the little girl had surpassed Elsbeth's expectations. "She seems to remember what she's already learned with a great deal of accuracy."

"Shame her parents are coming back sooner than they'd planned," the nurse murmured, shaking her head. "Only a fortnight and they'll be back to claim her."

Elsbeth froze, her hand on the chalk. "Oh?"

The nurse chuckled. "Don't you look so concerned. I know that Lord Radford had already made arrangements for you. You'll have a job to go to."

Shaking her head, Elsbeth stood up straight. "I don't think that's true, Mrs. Simpson."

"Of course, it is!" the older lady exclaimed with a laugh. "I've been given permission to talk to you about the girl since I'm the one who took care of her for Lord Radford in the first place."

Sitting down slowly, Elsbeth's stomach began to churn as she looked into the smiling face of Mrs. Simpson. "So, it is true," she murmured, half to herself. Lord Radford had said something about having another charge for her to care for, but she'd never truly believed him.

"Course it's true," Mrs. Simpson chuckled. "I'm sure you've heard all the rumors going about the place, but the truth is that Lord Radford is taking care of this young thing for his own good reasons. Reasons I can't explain."

Shaking her head to clear her dizzying thoughts, Elsbeth tried to smile at Mrs. Simpson, trying not to show her confusion. "Might you start at the beginning, Mrs. Simpson? I am not quite sure what you are speaking of."

Mrs. Simpson nodded patiently. "Of course. Rumors never help matters, as far as I'm concerned."

"I haven't heard any rumors," Elsbeth replied, firmly. "I'm the governess, which means the staff isn't all that keen to talk to me." That was one of the difficulties of being in her position. She was neither the level of the staff nor of the lord of the house, which meant that, aside from the nurse, she had very few people to talk to.

"Ah, yes. Of course," Mrs. Simpson murmured. "Well, I don't mind telling you that Lord Radford has been doing his utmost to keeping this charge of his as a closely guarded secret but, as it always is with staff, there are plenty of rumors flying about." She gave a slight shrug. "Not that anyone has the truth, however, which is just as Lord Radford wants it."

"The child," Elsbeth said, a touch impatiently. "Is the knowledge of her presence kept secret due to the fact that it might harm Lord Radford's reputation in some way? Does he think that he might have less influence with the ladies of the *ton* if they knew the truth about him?"

Mrs. Simpson laughed and shook her head. "Not in the least, Miss Blakely! Think of what you know of Lord Radford and tell me, do you truly believe that he will be harmed by such a thing? Or that, even if he was, he would care?"

The answer was already plain for her to see. "No, of course not," Elsbeth replied, with a slightly dark look. "I can imagine that he would not care a jot. I suppose then, it must be for the child's sake." That too went completely against what she knew of Lord Radford, believing him to be nothing more than a selfish, egotistical gentleman who cared nothing for others – but to her surprise, Mrs. Simpson nodded slowly.

"It surprised me also, to hear of it, but that is the truth," she said slowly, seeing Elsbeth's surprise. "It is more than just the child he is protecting by keeping the knowledge of her presence to himself as much as he can, but in due course, I know that he plans to do all he can for her."

"How do you know?" Elsbeth asked, frowning slightly. "I do not understand. I thought you were Miss Sarah's nurse."

"I am," Mrs. Simpson replied, with a small smile. "But before she came along, I was sent to Lord Radford's estate, to look after the child until other arrangements could be made. It was only for a short time, you understand, for my duty was to the Lord Radford's brother and his then expecting wife, but it was a lovely few months. I am sure you will find the girl to be a very sweet child."

Elsbeth nodded slowly, her brow furrowing as she thought about what Mrs. Simpson had said. "So I am to be sent to the Radford Estate to care for this child instead of Miss Sarah," she said quietly, her eyes still lingering on the smiling face of Mrs. Simpson. "I will be truthful with you and say that when first Lord Radford mentioned it to me, I thought him to be making up the whole scenario."

Mrs. Simpson chuckled. "Which I can well understand, my dear," she replied, with a broad smile. "Lord Radford is not the best of gentlemen, which I can see you are well aware of. However, I have heard that these last few days have seen him quite out of character, although I do not know why." She gave Elsbeth a small shrug before getting to her feet. "Perhaps it means that finally he is willing to take on the duties of his title, as he ought," she finished, shaking her head. "I have often heard his brother complain about Lord Radford's lack of duty to the title."

Elsbeth got to her feet and followed Mrs. Simpson to the door. "Thank you for coming to speak to me about this, Mrs. Simpson," she said, gratefully. "I have been quite at a loss this last week, not knowing what is to become of me when Miss Sarah returns home. It is a relief to know that I will have somewhere to go instead of being sent back to Smithfield House – should they be willing to accept me back!"

Mrs. Simpson patted Elsbeth's hand. "I am glad to have been of service to you, Miss Blakely. I will miss your company, although our acquaintance has been short, and wish you every happiness in your new post."

Elsbeth found herself smiling, relieved that she was not to be thrown into Lord Radford's path to be used as he pleased. She trusted Mrs. Simpson implicitly, which meant that the child *did* exist and that her role as governess was, in fact, to continue. "Thank you, Mrs. Simpson."

Closing the door behind the lady, Elsbeth wandered to the window of the schoolroom, looking out across the small gardens that lay at the back of the townhouse. She had not expected to hear such a thing from Mrs. Simpson, still believing that Lord Radford had made the whole situation up to calm her fears that he would try and claim her as his mistress once his niece had gone home. Now, it seemed, he had been telling her the truth.

Not that this was cause to trust him completely, for one truth in the midst of a whole muddle of manipulations, coercion and outright impropriety did not make his character any the better in her eyes.

As she was thinking this, her eyes fell on none other than Lord Radford himself, who appeared to be meandering through the gardens with no purposeful direction. He was moving slowly, his head down and his shoulders slumped. A picture of misery.

Elsbeth was unable to prevent herself from watching him, finding him to appear very different from the gentleman she had first met. He did not appear to be in a good frame of mind, given the downcast demeanor, and she could not help but wonder what was the matter.

Shaking her head, Elsbeth tried to turn away from him, tried not to allow her eyes to linger on him any longer but found that she could not help herself. She had so many questions about him, confused as to who Lord Radford really was and whether anything he had said to her about what her words had done to him could truly be trusted.

Her mind screamed at her to stay away from him, to reject every single word he said, and refuse to believe a single sentiment, and yet her heart could not forget the agony in his eyes when he'd looked at her and confessed that her brutal honesty had torn his heart.

On top of which, he had not come near her in the last week, dropping his attentions from her completely. She had expected him to send for her almost immediately, so that he might begin to press her again, but instead she had been waiting – and that in itself had unsettled her.

"Unless he is simply waiting until I begin to believe him," she muttered to herself, unable to prevent her distrust from rising again. "Only to pounce when I least expect it."

To her horror, Lord Radford then looked up at the window where she stood, as if he'd heard her speak. Their eyes met and Elsbeth found herself unable to move, staring down at Lord Radford as he stared up at her. Her cheeks mounted with color, wondering what he must think to see her watching him.

And then, he beckoned her down.

She stumbled away from the window at that, her heart quickening in her chest. He had beckoned her, wanting her to come down to him in the gardens, and now she had no choice but to do as he asked.

But the gardens? A place hidden from the staff, where Lord Radford might be alone? That was not the wisest place for her to go, given that she was still suspicious of his motives.

And yet, she knew she was obliged to do as he asked. She had already agreed to converse with him whenever he asked it of her, and now he would be waiting for her to attend him. A shudder shook her body as she picked up her shawl and wrapped it tightly around her shoulders. She was afraid.

Her legs were still shaking by the time she reached the gardens, stepping out through the wide-open doors and looking all around for Lord Radford.

"Ah, Miss Blakely. I wasn't sure you would come."

She twisted around to see him approaching her from the left, emerging from a pile of bushes which seemed to hide a small path. Her mouth went dry as he came closer, her heart beating frantically.

"Thank you for doing so," he continued, when she said nothing. "I am aware that I have not sent for you since our last conversation but, as I believe I said to you at the time, I have had a great deal to think about."

She managed a tight smile, still fearful about his intentions. "Yes, I remember, my lord."

He frowned, the light fading from his expression. "You do not look particularly at ease, Miss Blakely. Is everything quite all right?"

Her arms still folded tightly about her chest, Elsbeth nodded jerkily. "Of course."

"You have nothing to fear from me any longer, Miss Blakely," he said softly, still standing a good distance away from her. "I mean to prove to you that I am intent on changing my ways. You have been the impetus I needed to set me on an entirely new path and I confess that I feel indebted to you for that."

Swallowing hard, Elsbeth studied Lord Radford's open expression, seeing no hint of the arrogance she'd expected to see there.

"You will not believe me straight away, of course, which I quite understand," he continued, with a small sigh. "But I will prove it to you, if you will allow me the opportunity. I want to ensure that you are well taken care of and that you are able to fulfill your role as you ought, without fear from me or from anyone else. I will no longer be pushing you as I once thought to do, for I realize now that this was quite wrong of me. In fact, I realize that there is a great deal wrong with how I have been living my life these past few years – which I will not go into at this present moment for fear of boring you." He chuckled, and, to Elsbeth's surprise, she found her lips curving into a small smile in return.

"Mrs. Simpson spoke to me of your charge," she said when he smiled back at her. "I confess that I did not believe her to be real."

"She is very real, Miss Blakely," Lord Radford replied, with another wide grin. "And has everyone in my staff under her command, as I am sure you will soon see. That is, of course, so long as you are still willing to come to my home and be the governess to Miss Amy?"

"Miss Amy?"

He nodded. "Did I not tell you? I do apologize. Her name is Amy and she is only a few months older than Miss Sarah.

"I see," Elsbeth murmured, her mind beginning to fill

with questions over the young girl. "And she is *your* charge?"

Lord Radford glanced at her, frowning. "She is not from my loins, if that is what you are thinking, Miss Blakely."

Elsbeth felt herself blush as she looked away, wondering how he'd been able to read her thoughts.

"And yet I can understand why you might think so," he continued, a little more heavily. "I will not divulge all, but regardless, the child needs a governess. Will you take up the post, Miss Blakely? It would mean a great deal to me if you would."

"You are giving me the choice, Lord Radford?" Unable to hide her surprise, Elsbeth stared at the gentleman in front of her, a little unsure as to why he would consider giving her the option to refuse.

A wry smile touched his lips. "After how badly I have treated you, Miss Blakely, I hardly think it right or fair of me to demand that you do as I ask. You have every reason to distrust me."

"And yet you know that I have very little option but to remain with you," she said slowly, still doubting him. "Where else could I go?"

He sighed and looked away. "I would not have you out on the streets even though I know you would do as well as you could there. If you truly do not wish to remain with me and come to the Radford Estate, then I will make sure you have a new position to go to."

Her mouth fell open, her breath gone from her as she saw the sincerity in his eyes. This could not have been anything but the truth, she realized, seeing that he was determined to do right by her. There was to be no more of his chasing, no more of his determined advances. He had been telling her the truth, her words *had* somehow had a profound effect on him.

And now she had the chance to leave his house and his company forever.

"I know that Lord and Lady Dalrymple plan to advertise for a suitable governess for their somewhat precocious son, Miss Blakely," Lord Radford finished, with another small smile. "I am sure you would do very well there."

"Might I think about it, Lord Radford?"

He smiled. "Well, at least that is not an outright refusal to stay in your post. Yes, of course, Miss Blakely. I will gladly give you all the time you require with this."

"Miss Sarah is to leave us very soon, I understand," Elsbeth responded, finding it hard to know how to react to this new Lord Radford, finding him so very different from how he had been with her before. "Might I think over things until then?" She held her breath, seeing the intensity in his gaze as he studied her for a long moment, before finally nodding.

"But of course, Miss Blakely. That would suit me very well."

She nodded, her fingers tightening as she clasped her hands together, suddenly filled with a nervous tension – although she did not say from where it came. Was it because Lord Radford was behaving so very differently to before? Or was it merely because she was close to him and still afraid that he might, somehow, reach for her in a most inappropriate manner?

"Thank you, my lord," she managed to say, trying to hide her confusion. "Might I be excused?"

He nodded. "Certainly. And thank you, Miss Blakely. I look forward to hearing your response very soon."

CHAPTER EIGHT

Two Weeks Later

"Whatever is the matter with you, old boy?"

Andrew let out a long, frustrated breath as he turned his gaze onto his friend, Lord Watson.

"I will have you know that, for the umpteenth time, there is nothing wrong with me. In fact, things are going very well. Why do you ask?" He sat back in his chair and ordered another brandy, thinking to himself that Whites was growing rather dull of late. He had always enjoyed being a part of the gentlemen's club, but recently he had found the conversation boring and the company even more staid. Lord Watson, who had been a longtime friend of his, seemed to care about nothing but talking of Andrew's own behavior, apparently finding his change in character to be nothing short of fascinating.

"You need to leave it alone, Watson," Andrew muttered, as Lord Watson opened his mouth to speak.

"Nothing is the matter with me. I am not touched in the head, nor am I almost done in. I am quite healthy and as fit as a fiddle. I simply intend to take on my duties as the titled member of the family."

"But that has never bothered you before!" Lord Watson protested, his hand gripping the brandy glass tightly as he stared at Andrew in confusion. "Why the sudden change of heart? One day you are throwing yourself into whatever pleasures you can, only to turn away from them all the following afternoon! That makes very little sense, Lord Radford, which begs me to ask the question as to whether or not you are quite well!"

"I *am* quite well," Andrew retorted, firmly. "For goodness sake, Watson, leave it be. If you want to know the truth, what I will simply say is that someone has finally been able to show me my true self and I have found him to be severely wanting." Shaking his head, he recalled how Miss Blakely had been so harsh and yet so honest with him in what she'd said, as though she'd held up a mirror so that he might see his face. It had been a startling moment, a moment when he'd struggled to think clearly as his mind refused to accept what was being said, only for him then to have his world torn into shreds around him.

Miss Blakely had put him in his place and, for managing to do such a thing, she was worth keeping in his household.

But you gave her the choice, remember?

Frowning, Andrew shook his head, aware that he still had not received an answer from the lady even though Miss Sarah had been carted off by her father this morning. He had seen very little of Miss Blakely over the last fortnight and had made every effort to steer clear of her when he did. It was as if he was doing his utmost to prove to both her and himself that he truly *was* a man who was slowly becoming a reformed character. The truth was, he wanted her to stay. He had taken her into his confidence with regard to Miss Amy and prayed to goodness that she didn't either listen to or believe the rumors that she might hear from the staff. Of course, they all knew that to speak a word about Miss Amy to anyone outside the house was to bring down his rage upon them and, so, he had been able to keep the girl's presence in his home almost secret. Not that he regretted telling Miss Blakely, he just hoped that she would decide to come with him to his estate, if only to mend the deep gulf that had opened up between them.

"There's a lady, is that it?"

Drawn back into conversation, Andrew looked over at Lord Watson, seeing the man grinning almost maniacally.

"A lady?" he repeated, snorting with distain. "I have no intentions as regards any ladies, Watson. You'd be best to close your mouth before you get yourself into trouble.

Lord Watson chuckled loudly, which to Andrew's relief was drowned out by the many other conversations that were going on all around them. He wanted to curl up into a ball so that no one else could see him, desperate for Lord Watson to be silent.

"Then why do you wish to give up all of this?!" Lord Watson exclaimed, gesturing to the crowd of gentlemen now gathered there. "You do not play cards any longer, you will not gamble. You don't go out on the town with the rest of us when we need to visit a less than proper establishment, those 'ladies of the night' as we call them. Instead, you either sit at home or go to some event or other where you might behave as jovially as the rest of them before going back to your own bed! My goodness, man! Whatever has become of you? It's like I do not know you anymore."

Much to Lord Watson's confusion, his last comment brought Andrew a great deal of delight, pushing away his irritation. If his friend did not know him any longer, then that could only mean that his change in character had been a genuine one. Neither did it bring Andrew any frustration that he was no longer the man Lord Watson knew, finding himself growing more and more delighted with that notion.

"You are a lost cause, old boy," Lord Watson muttered, throwing back his drink. "And you are gone from town in three days' time?"

"Indeed, I am," Andrew replied, still wondering if Miss Blakely would come with him or remain in his townhouse until he had found her a new position. "Responsibilities, and all that."

Lord Watson groaned. "And now you are leaving just when things are starting to get interesting around here."

"Interesting?" Andrew repeated, with a note of curiosity in his voice. "What's happened, Watson? Do not tell me some cock and bull story that is nothing but made up nonsense in an attempt to keep me here for I do not wish to hear it!"

Lord Watson muttered something under his breath

before sighing heavily. "No, it appears I will not be able to keep you here regardless."

"Then what is it that was so interesting?" Andrew asked, laughing. "Not something to catch my attention, I presume?"

Lord Watson sighed heavily and passed a hand over his eyes, as though Andrew were wearying him terribly. "No, not too interesting, I suppose. It was only that I remembered you said that you went to that Smithfield House for Girls recently."

The smile was wiped from Andrew's face at once and he sat a little more upright in his chair. "Yes, I did," he murmured, frowning. "Why? Has something happened?"

Lord Watson shrugged. "Nothing terrible, but I did hear that a Duke had gone visiting."

Andrew stared at him. "A Duke?"

"From what I know, yes," Lord Watson replied, with a small smile. "See now, you are interested in such a thing! Why would you leave London when –"

"Stay on track, Watson," Andrew interrupted, firmly. "This Duke. Who was he?"

Lord Watson shrugged, hiding a wide yawn with the back of his hand. "Not quite sure. The only reason I know about this was because the lady who runs the place got into a terrible screaming match with the Duke inside the House for Girls. Apparently, someone called the constable to make sure she was all right, I think they thought someone was attacking her."

A peculiar sensation of urgency began to settle over Andrew as he listened, somehow believing that this was to do with Miss Blakely in some way, although he could not say where such a thought had come from.

"A Miss Skelton, I think the man said," Lord Watson finished, looking at Andrew with a slightly concerned expression. "Are you all right, man? You look quite done in all of a sudden."

"I'm fine, thank you," Andrew muttered, sitting back in his chair and trying to think clearly. "A Duke, you say? Are you quite sure?"

"I'm sure I know what that old friend of mine said, and he watched the whole thing!" Lord Watson exclaimed. "Duke of Bartonshire or something, I can't be certain what."

"A shouting match with Miss Skelton," Andrew murmured, a knot of unease settling in him. "And that lady is not one to take anything lying down."

Lord Watson chuckled darkly. "So I've heard."

"And you really have very little idea as to what went on?"

"None!" Lord Watson exclaimed, his eyes lit with a flickering hope. "Does this mean, by any chance, that you might consider lingering in London for a time? I do hope so, old boy. I'm sure I can tempt you back into your old ways given time."

Shaking his head, Andrew got up from the table and patted Lord Watson on the shoulder. "Afraid not, Lord Watson. I am even more determined to leave this place in a few days' time. Although, do me a favor, would you? If you do hear any more, would you be able to write to me the details of whatever it is you have found out? I could make it worth your while since I know you find such labors terribly difficult." He made sure to add a note of mockery to his final words, making Lord Watson grimace.

"Yes, yes, you may laugh at my unwillingness when it comes to writing letters and the like but when it comes to you, of course I will do as you ask. Although, what did you have in mind by way of making it 'worth my while'?"

Andrew shrugged. "I could pay off your tab here?"

Lord Watson's eyes lit up. "Capital, Lord Radford, absolutely capital! For that, I should send you one letter a week!"

Chuckling, Andrew put on his hat and pulled on his gloves. "A letter a week then, Lord Watson. Make sure to have Whites send the bill to me and I will pay it directly, before I return home. Good evening."

"Good evening," Lord Watson replied, now seeming to be much less dejected than he had been before. The prospect of having his tab paid off seemed to have done him the world of good.

Still chuckling to himself at how easily Lord Watson had been placated, Andrew hailed a hackney and headed home, feeling rather in fine spirits. The prospect of leaving London had never felt so joyous and he found that he was rather looking forward to returning to his estate. Perhaps it was because he had finally seen himself for who he truly was and was now willing to set all his vices aside for the sake of becoming a dutiful, responsible viscount. He had to hope it was that, although he was quite sure that his mother, the Dowager Radford, would be delighted at the sudden change in him.

Once home, Andrew made his way to the library, intent on having a final drink before he retired. The butler and the rest of the staff had already gone to bed, which he was glad of, feeling as though he wanted to be entirely alone with his thoughts. What Lord Watson had said about the House for Girls, the mysterious Duke and Miss Skelton had rather unnerved him, for to hear that such a terrible commotion had gone on in the house had left him with a conclusion that, whilst shaky, was something he could not let go of.

This was all to do, somehow, with Miss Blakely. He could not say why or for what reason, but the strange way Miss Skelton had treated her had always given him pause, even when he had not cared about her other than something to satisfy his desires. Miss Blakely herself had talked about how Miss Skelton had pushed her away, done all she could to rid her from the House for Girls, but had never found out any explanation as to why that might have been.

Perhaps the Duke had something to do with it all.

Frowning to himself, Andrew poured himself a measure of brandy and sat down by the fire, seeing the small tray with two letters on it. The butler must have set it here for him, knowing that he usually spent a short time in the library on his return from whatever social occasion he had been at.

Picking them up, he saw that one was a letter and the other a small handwritten note. Opening the note, he scanned the few short lines, a broad smile spreading across his face.

'Lord Radford, I would be glad to join you at the Radford Estate and to teach Miss Amy. I do hope I have not left it too late. Miss Blakely.'

It was short and to the point and yet left Andrew with such a feeling of overwhelming delight that, for a long moment, he could not so much as drag his eyes away from it. Miss Blakely was going to come to take up her role as governess in his house. She had trusted him enough to accept. That brought him such a profound sense of relief that he did not quite know what to do with himself, his throat aching with a sudden sharp emotion.

Why do I feel this way?

The question had him stop dead, his smile fading and fingers gripping the paper tightly. Why did he care so much about Miss Blakely's presence at his Estate? After all, he had sworn to her that he would not go near her again, would not urge her to come to his bed as he had once planned, so why keep her so near to him when he knew that his desire for her, his interest in her, had not yet waned?

Even that in itself was cause for confusion. She had rebuffed him at every turn until he had seen himself in such a poor light that he had been forced to take stock – but still, his eyes still sought her out, his lips still curved into a smile whenever she drew near. He still found her intriguing, wondering about where she had come from, wondering about her life in the House for Girls. It no longer entered his mind that she was of much lower class than he, for he found her to be more than his equal. After all, none of his equals had ever spoken to him in the way she had done! She had more strength, more courage and sense of respect in her than any of his acquaintances. She knew what was merited her and she had stood up for it, casting his rank and status aside until he had been forced to fall to his knees and try to pick up the pieces of his life.

So what was he to do with these strange, tangling emotions that threaded through his heart whenever he saw her, or even thought of her? Was he to believe himself truly fond of the lady, even though they had only just set aside the past with the hopes of moving forward?

Groaning aloud, Andrew put his head in his hands, the paper crinkling as he did so. This was all much too confusing. He would simply be glad that Miss Blakely had decided to come to his Estate and teach Miss Amy. The rest, he would work out later.

Setting the crumpled note aside, Andrew picked up the letter and broke the seal, not quite sure where it had come from since he did not recognize it. To his surprise, he saw the address for the Smithfield House for Girls at the top, his stomach tightening with a sudden, fierce tension.

'My Lord Radford, I regret to inform you that Miss Blakely's presence is required back at the House for Girls with immediate effect. Please ensure that she is returned without delay. We will be, of course, recompensing you for any loss of income or the like. Sincerely, Miss A. Skelton, Smithfield House for Girls.'

His jaw clenched. His instincts had been quite right. Something was wrong at Smithfield house and it all centered around Miss Blakely, although he was quite sure she would be as at much of a loss as he.

He did not want to send her back, an urge to protect her growing steadily deeper as he re-read the letter. Of course, he should allow her to read the letter and make her choice, but what if she chose to return? It was not all that likely, of course, since he knew that she had been rather angry about how Miss Skelton had treated her, but regardless, there was still the chance that she would capitulate. Miss Skelton had manipulated her once and he was certain she could do it again.

How ashamed he was to remember that he had been a party to all of that.

He was not quite sure what to do with the letter, toying between throwing it in the flames and ignoring it altogether or finding Miss Blakely first thing in the morning and telling her everything about what he had heard from Lord Watson and then what he had read.

And then, before he could decide, the door opened and Miss Blakely, dressed in her night things, stepped into the room.

CHAPTER NINE

An involuntary shriek left Elsbeth's mouth as a figure in front of the fire moved, just as she stepped into the room. Grasping the door handle to steady herself, she held on tightly, only to hear Lord Radford's voice coming towards her.

"I do apologize, Miss Blakely, I did not mean to scare you."

Pulling the top of her dressing gown tightly against her throat, Elsbeth tried to calm her frantically beating heart, her eyes wide. "I do apologize, Lord Radford," she gasped, making to leave him alone again. "It was quite my mistake. I did not think you had returned and I could not sleep and so –"

"It is, in fact, rather fortuitous that you have arrived as you did," he said, calmly. "Might you step inside for a moment? I have something of importance to tell you."

She hesitated, her mind screaming at her to run away from him, particularly when she was dressed in her night things – although they covered her just as well as any governess' gown.

"I do not think –"

"I will not rise from my chair," he promised, evidently aware of what she was going to say. "I swear it to you, my dear lady. Come now, you have trusted me thus far, can you not trust me just a little more?"

It was on the tip of Elsbeth's tongue to say that she did not trust him very much at all but, calming herself, she let go of the door handle with an effort and stepped inside.

"It is to do with the Smithfield House for Girls, Miss Blakely," Lord Radford said, as she sat down. "I am not quite sure what to make of it all but my instincts tell me that all is not well there."

Hearing the worry in his voice, Elsbeth frowned as he held out a letter to her, taking it from him at once. Her fingers jerked away from his as they brushed but, with a small sigh of relief, she saw that he had not noticed.

No, she certainly was not entirely comfortable around this gentleman as yet.

"Read it and then I shall tell you more," Lord Radford said, encouragingly. "There is not a lot there but there is enough to make it highly significant."

A trifle confused, Elsbeth let her eyes turn to the letter in her hand, reading the few short lines with increasing concern. She had no idea as to why her presence would be required back at the Smithfield House, feeling as though she was, once again, simply a toy to be used by those who required her.

"It is very odd, is it not?" came Lord Radford's murmur. "I cannot imagine what Miss Skelton means to achieve in demanding such a thing."

Caught with a sudden fear, Elsbeth looked up at him in fright. "Do you mean to....?"

He leaned forward, his eyes warm in the firelight. "Do not concern yourself in that regard, my dear lady. I have no thought of returning you there. In fact, I was battling between throwing it in the fire and ignoring it altogether or allowing it to be your decision." He gave her a small smile, which calmed her frantic nerves. "It appears that you are to make the choice yourself."

The thought of returning to the Smithfield House for Girls made her almost queasy, her stomach tightening as she clung to the arm of the chair with one hand as though to steady herself.

"My offer to have you as governess to Miss Amy still stands, Miss Blakely," Lord Radford murmured. "You have no requirement to do as they ask since you are no longer their charge. The moment you left the premises, you became your own person."

It did not feel like that, however, and Elsbeth was forced to battle her doubts, suddenly worried that there was something wrong with Mrs. Banks or the like.

"I should also tell you that one of my friends, Lord Watson, had heard some news about your House for Girls."

She looked up at him, seeing his concern.

"There is more?"

Shrugging, he let his eyes drift to the letter. "Perhaps I should have told you this first. My friend, Lord Watson, told me that he heard a Duke had visited Smithfield House. I'm afraid he could not quite remember the name – one of the consequences of too much brandy, I'm afraid – but he did remember that there had been a constable called to the House."

Gripped by terror, she leaned forward, her eyes wide. "Do tell me that nothing is wrong with Mrs. Banks?"

He frowned, reaching forward to take her hand in his warm one. "No, my dear Miss Blakely, there is nothing about her as far as I know."

She let out a long, shaky breath, feeling tears prick at the corner of her eyes. For a moment, she had been convinced that something dreadful had happened to Mrs. Banks, her one steadfast friend, and given Miss Skelton's threats as regarded her, it was nothing but sheer relief to know that she was not involved in anything.

"No, Miss Blakely, you need not worry about her," Lord Radford continued, gently. "My friend, Lord Watson, said that a constable had been called due to all the screaming that was coming from the place. There was no one hurt, you understand, but it was, in fact, a shouting match between this Duke and Miss Skelton."

"An argument?" Elsbeth repeated, blinking in confusion. "They were shouting so loudly that someone thought there was a beating or the like?"

"Something like that, yes," Lord Radford replied, with a rueful smile. "The constable did not say what the argument was about, but truth be told, Miss Blakely, I am concerned that this letter arriving so soon after this incident means that the two are tied together."

A stone dropped into her belly. She had not thought

to make the connection, having been overwhelmed with thoughts of the letter, but Lord Radford was quite right to suggest such a thing.

"Do you wish to return to Smithfield House, Miss Blakely?" Lord Radford asked, gently. "I will do whatever it is you require of me, for this must be your choice."

She swallowed the lump in her throat, terror filling her. She did not know what this letter meant, for it gave no indication as to *why* she was required back there, but she knew she could not return. As much as she loved Mrs. Banks and missed her terribly, there was nothing that could induce her to return to Miss Skelton.

"No, Lord Radford, I do not wish to return," she replied firmly, looking at him. "In fact, I would be glad if you would throw this letter into the flames and let it burn. Let it be as though it was never delivered, as though we have never read the words contained within. I cannot imagine going back there again." She set her shoulders, feeling a great deal more at rest now that she had made her decision. "I am, as you say, a free person and can choose not to go when I am summoned," she finished, suddenly aware that their hands were still joined. "Thank you for reminding me of that, Lord Radford."

Letting go of his hand, she handed him back the letter and, as he took it, she felt herself caught by the look in his eyes. He was simply watching her, taking her in, but there was such a tenderness about his expression that she found she could not look away. She did not know what to make of it, nor of the way her heart began to quicken as though delighted with his attentions.

"A very good choice, Miss Blakely," Lord Radford murmured, crumpling the letter up into his hand before throwing it into the flames. "I know that I would have missed your presence should you have chosen to return."

There was nothing she could say in response, astonished at the openness of both his voice and his words. They had not spent a great deal of time together and yet, here he was telling her that he would find her absence to be something of a trial to him! Seeing him watch the letter being licked up by the flames, Elsbeth let her gaze travel over him for a few moments longer, seeing him in such a different light from before. It was a transformation that was taking place before her very eyes. Here she was beginning to feel safe and secure, allowing herself to trust him little by little.

"I think perhaps we should travel to the Estate tomorrow, Miss Blakely," he said, as he turned his head to smile at her. "What say you to that?"

She could not help but smile back at him, her heart lifting with relief. "I think that a very good notion, Lord Radford," she replied, gently. "The less time I have to spend in London, the better, I think."

He chuckled. "I could not agree more, Miss Blakely. Tomorrow it is."

Walking back to her room, her mind still full and her hands still empty of the book she had gone in search of, Elsbeth was forced to reflect on the man who was her employer. She had not expected such kindness from him, such understanding, but yet here he was, doing more for her than she had ever expected. Recalling how Lord

Radford had been grasping, arrogant and entirely self-centered, Elsbeth found that she could not reconcile that with the man she knew now. It had not yet been a fortnight since she had reprimanded him so fiercely and yet she was convinced that the change in him was a genuine one.

Opening her door and stepping into her room, Elsbeth let out a long breath of relief, a small smile touching her lips. She felt as though she had achieved something of great importance in asking Lord Radford to throw the letter onto the fire, seeing the words Miss Skelton had written being licked up by the flames. She would not be summoned as though she belonged to Miss Skelton, as though she were a servant who could be treated with such disdain.

"I do not have to think of her again," she murmured to herself, walking to the window and looking out at the quiet London streets, seeing the way the moonlight bounced off the cobbles. "Never again."

The happiness in her soul was suddenly pulled from her as a figure detached itself from the shadows that clung to the side of the street and ambled towards the house, a small lamp in one hand. Her breath caught, even though she had no reason to fear that this figure was in any way threatening. A feeling of unease began to settle over her as she continued to look out of the window, seeing the figure stop only a few feet away from the house. Not quite certain what to make of the shadowy figure who appeared to be watching the house, Elsbeth made to move away from the window, only for the figure to lift his lantern high into the air, as though to attempt to see what she was doing.

Stumbling away from the window, Elsbeth pressed one hand to her chest, feeling her heart pounding rapidly. This was no coincidence, she was sure of it. That man, whoever he was, had been watching the house – perhaps even watching her room to see where she went and what she was doing. With no drapes on her window, which was not a surprise given her position here, she had no way of hiding herself from him.

"But why?" she breathed, her legs trembling and forcing her to sit down on her bed. "Why is someone watching me?"

Putting her head in her hands, Elsbeth tried to make sense of it all, but found herself pulled lower and lower into the mire of confusion. A Duke at Smithfield House for Girls, an argument between him and Miss Skelton, the letter demanding her return to the House and now a man watching Lord Radford's home, watching *her* window?

For a moment, Elsbeth fought the urge to get out of her chair and make her way straight to the House for Girls, the desperation to know what it was all about almost possessing her completely. She did not like being kept in the dark; she wanted to know *why* Miss Skelton had demanded her return, yet found herself recoiling from the very idea.

"If I go back there, I might never come out again," she said softly, her hands slowly loosening as she sat back up again. She could not return. She would do as she had said and go with Lord Radford to his estate to meet her new charge. That would satisfy her completely, even if she never learned why Miss Skelton had demanded her return. In a few years' time, she would have her freedom and she could put all this behind her.

Steeling her resolve, Elsbeth rose to her feet, found an old bedraggled blanket that lay in the corner by her bed and, her heart beating in her throat, threw it over the top of the old curtain rail that sat above the window. It would not give her much protection from the man's view when the sun came up, but it would be better than nothing. Lifting a corner of the blanket, she looked out of the window once more, seeing the small flickering light that glowed in the middle of the street. He was still there. Still watching. Still as troubling as before.

Swallowing hard, Elsbeth drew in a long breath and tried to calm her anxiety. The man could not get into Lord Radford's home, and she would speak to him about it as soon as she could.

Lying down on her bed, Elsbeth tried to close her eyes and drift off to sleep, tugging the blankets up to her chin. Drawing in a long breath, she let it out slowly, trying to force herself to relax. She was safe here, she told herself, safe in Lord Radford's home and under his protection – although not in the way he had anticipated! She allowed herself a small smile as she thought of how carefully he had held her hand, how he had tried so hard to reassure her. He had been her anchor as she'd been tossed here and there, confused as to what Miss Skelton was doing. Despite her worries, she knew that he would protect her for as long as she was willing to remain in his employment. Even that, she knew, was her choice, for

Lord Radford would not demand her presence as he had done before. Even though she was to be the governess for his ward, Elsbeth knew that she still had the freedom to either stay or to leave whenever she felt the time was right. In that way he had ensured her independence, and Elsbeth felt herself growing all the more grateful for that.

CHAPTER TEN

"Finally," Andrew muttered to himself as he kicked his horse into a gallop up the driveway, his heart lifting to see his home once more. It was vastly unusual for him to feel such delight over his estate, when he was usually much more at home in London, but for whatever reason, knowing that Miss Blakely was to be in his home alongside him brought him such happiness that he could not feel even a modicum of discontent.

Glancing behind him, he saw the carriage turn in, his lips lifting with the smallest of smiles as he thought of Miss Blakely kept within. She had turned out to be a rather interesting companion, for he had asked to sit with her in the carriage during their long journey to the Radford Estate when his horse had grown tired, and she had been more than obliging. Of course, he had ensured there was a maid in the carriage also – but she was asleep for most of their conversations and so Andrew had barely noticed her.

However, one thing troubled him immensely. The

fact that Miss Blakely had been certain there had been a man watching her window. It was not that he did not believe her, for he was quite sure that the lady would not lie about something so grave, but his heart grew worried over the reason for such a strange presence to be watching Miss Blakely. He had offered to send a man to London in order to find out and, after a moment of hesitation, she had agreed. Andrew was to write to his London steward almost the moment he returned to the estate, determined to put an end to the confusion and worry that wrapped itself around Miss Blakely's shoulders. He himself could make no sense of it, his mind scrambling between ideas as he tried to find some simple conclusion to explain it away. However, the only conclusion he could come to was that the Duke, the House for Girls and Miss Blakely were all, somehow, tied together, but that he did not particularly want to find out why. As far as he was concerned, Miss Blakely now belonged here and that was all that mattered.

Jumping down from his horse, Andrew tossed the reins to the waiting groom before letting out a long sigh of relief.

He was home. Miss Blakely would be more than safe here.

"Radford?"

Turning around to the front door, Andrew bit back a gasp of surprise to see his mother, Lady Agatha Radford, standing with her hands on her hips. Her grey hair was piled neatly on her head, with one delicate peacock feather rising from the back of it, giving her an almost regal appearance. Her face was sheet white, making Andrew wonder whether or not she was altogether well.

"Mother," he managed to say, just as the carriage rolled up the driveway. "How good to see you. I didn't expect..."

"No, I know you did not, but I came regardless," she replied, coming down the stairs towards him. "Your brother has told me everything."

He swallowed hard, the reason for her pallor suddenly obvious.

"I – I do not know what to say, Andrew."

There was a softness in her voice, a look in her eyes that took Andrew by surprise. She had not spoken to him with such tenderness in a long time, leaving him with a surprising sense of warmth towards her.

"Mother," he said softly, coming closer to her. "It was a burden you did not have to carry. It was for the best. I am only sorry that you had to find out in such an abrupt fashion."

The lady swallowed hard, her eyes shining with sparkling tears and yet a small smile lingered on her lips. "I did not think there was that kind of good in you, Andrew. Forgive me for being so disillusioned with you."

He shook his head, just as the footman moved to open the carriage door. "Mother, you have every right to think of me as you do – or as you did. I only did this in order to spare the family shame, and not because I truly had any interest in helping my brother. However, I would like to tell you now that I have seen myself for who I truly am and that the reflection that peered back at me was one that I disliked intensely." His throat suddenly ached and he shook his head, finding it difficult to speak for a moment, such was the intensity of his emotions. "Miss Blakely has been the one to show me my character for what it truly is, and I want you to greet her with all kindness and favor, Mother. She is to be Miss Amy's governess."

His mother took his hand and held it tightly, not looking towards Miss Blakely as she descended from the carriage. "This governess has brought about such a change in you, Radford?" Her lips thinned and Andrew could see the worry in her eyes. "And now you have brought her here?"

Andrew gave his mother a half smile, aware of what she thought of him. "Miss Blakely is nothing more than a well-respected young lady, Mother. In fact, you might be glad to know that it is because she would not do as I wished that I was first shown my true self. I realized that I was selfish and arrogant, expecting everyone to do as I wanted and as I asked without a thought for their own wellbeing. Her character is one of pure gold, Mother, and I am sure you will see that for yourself."

"But as a governess, it is not as though we will see much of her," his mother protested, her standing as a Dowager Viscountess coming into play as she considered the gap between their stations. "Surely, Radford –"

Patting her hand, Andrew cut her off. "Mother, this will be a strange situation for you, but I fully intend to have Miss Blakely dine with us, sit with us and be treated as a guest in our home, despite the fact that she will have duties and responsibilities as a hired member of my staff. There is something more to her, something that I have not yet worked out nor understand, but believe me, there is a need for her to be treated with friendship and compassion." He kept his voice low, aware that Miss Blakely was still standing by the carriage, waiting to be summoned. "She comes from the Smithfield House for Girls, Mother, but there is more to her story than meets the eye. A Duke may be searching for her, as may the lady who runs the House for Girls, but for whatever reason, we cannot be sure. Miss Blakely is aware of this and has chosen to come here, to turn her back on the House for Girls and this potential Duke. There was someone watching her, Mother, and for that reason, I cannot help but feel the need to protect her."

His mother looked back at him steadily, her green eyes as sharp as they had ever been – to the point that Andrew felt as though they were looking into his very soul.

"I have never heard you speak of another living soul with such concern, Radford," she said eventually, her words slow and careful. "Whether or not this is a genuine change, I cannot help but be grateful for it. I will be glad to meet Miss Blakely and, regardless of whether or not I feel comfortable with the situation you propose, I will go along with it. You are, after all, the lord of this estate now and as such, I will defer to your judgment."

Andrew swallowed the lump in his throat, aware that his mother had not shown him this kind of respect before. Not that he had ever deserved it before, of course, but this was more than he had ever expected, or had ever merited.

"Thank you, Mother," he murmured, before turning towards Miss Blakely. "Miss Blakely, might you come over here, please? I would like to introduce you to my mother, the Dowager Lady Radford."

Miss Blakely blushed as she came over to greet Lady Radford, her eyes on the ground as she curtsied beautifully, murmuring a word of greeting. Andrew could not help but feel a curl of tension in his belly as he looked at his mother, wondering what her reaction would be to Miss Blakely.

"You have had a great influence on my son, I hear, Miss Blakely," Lady Radford replied, as Miss Blakely stood up again. "And are to be governess to Miss Amy."

"I am," Miss Blakely replied, quietly. "I do hope that I can fulfill the role given to me by Lord Radford."

The Dowager nodded slowly. "I am sure you will, Miss Blakely. And in the meantime, I hear we are to spend some time together over the course of my visit here. I look forward to becoming a little better acquainted with you."

Andrew felt Miss Blakely's eyes land on him, saw her astonishment, and managed to give a small shrug. "I have told my mother your current situation and all that has gone on of late," he said, by way of explanation. "It is my desire that you dine with us each evening and join us afterward for some conversation and that like."

Her face burned with color. "Lord Radford, that is not necessary, I assure you. I am more than aware that it is not my place and do not wish you to feel obliged in any way towards me. Not when you have been so kind already."

He shook his head, aware that he had not been all that kind to Miss Blakely but had, in fact, been something of a tyrant. "Miss Blakely, I will not have it any other way. In fact, I shall insist. We are in the country and, as it is, no one will comment on your company with us. I would not have you spend each evening alone, worrying about what news might come from London."

Her eyes met his and, caught by the beauty of them, Andrew's breath hitched, leaving him unable to continue his speech for a moment. She was smiling at him, her expression open and eyes warm, looking at him in such a way that he wanted to drag her into his arms and crush her tight against him, promising to look after her for the rest of her days if she would but let him.

"Then shall we step inside?"

His mother's voice broke through his fog of desire, pushing away the clouds and setting him back to reality. He could not do such a thing, not in front of his mother and certainly not when Miss Blakely had only just begun to trust him.

"Indeed," he said, clearing his throat. "Miss Blakely, I shall introduce you to Miss Amy and then leave you to settle into your rooms. Do join us for dinner, however. I think it best that I tell you the truth about Miss Amy and her situation here."

She nodded, her smile fading as she caught sight of the Dowager's steely gaze.

"It is for the best, Mother," he said softly, aware of the concern in his mother's eyes. "Miss Blakely can be trusted. You need have no doubt about that."

"Very well," his mother murmured, still not looking altogether pleased. "Then I shall see you this evening, Miss Blakely. Good afternoon."

Miss Blakely curtsied again as Lady Radford made her way back up the steps towards the house, leaving Andrew standing by Miss Blakely's side.

"My mother surprised me with her visit, but I do not think that it is altogether a bad thing," he murmured, offering Miss Blakely his arm without even realizing he was doing it. "We may find that we require her counsel."

Miss Blakely looked up at him, glancing at his arm for a moment before accepting it. Andrew felt his body burst to life as they walked up the steps together, aware that he felt more for Miss Blakely than he ought.

"I am looking forward to meeting Miss Amy and beginning my life here, Lord Radford," Miss Blakely said quietly, as they walked into the entrance hall. "I feel very blessed to have been allowed to come here. You have been very good to me."

Smiling down at her, Andrew saw the wonderment in her eyes as she took in his home. "It is nothing less than you deserve, after how I treated you, Miss Blakely," he said, softly. "The fact that you are so willing and able to trust me is more than I ever hoped for. If I may be so bold, I am glad to have you here with me, Miss Blakely. I do not think I could have left you behind in London."

Her eyes met his as their steps came to a sudden stop, simply looking into each other's face with nothing being said between them. Andrew did not know what to say or what to do, feeling as though Miss Blakely almost belonged here, growing pained at the thought of ushering her into the governess' rooms instead of to the room that adjoined his. It was not as though he simply wanted her in his bed any longer, but that he wanted her to be a permanent part of his life. Now that she was here, he did not want her to leave again, nor did he want her merely to be Miss Amy's governess.

Confusion swirled through his mind as they looked at one another, nothing but silence surrounding them. Her breath tickled across as he leaned down just a little, finding himself so drawn to her that he could do nothing more.

And then the excited giggle of a small child echoed through the house, breaking the silence between them. Miss Blakely looked all around her, a smile spreading across her face as her hand tightened on his arm.

"Miss Amy, I presume?" she whispered, as though not wanting to interrupt the laughter that still echoed around them. "She sounds like a very happy child."

Andrew smiled a little ruefully, somewhat frustrated that they had been interrupted, whilst also being a little relieved that the moment had passed without him feeling the need to act. Whatever it was between them, he couldn't let himself fall back into old habits, not without being sure that what he felt was real – and sure that Miss Blakely would react with pleasure instead of anger towards any expression of those feelings.

"She is very happy," he replied, softly, turning towards the staircase. "Come now, let me introduce her to you."

CHAPTER ELEVEN

Elsbeth felt the last of her trepidation melt away as dessert was placed in front of her, glad that the Dowager now appeared to be at ease with her company at the dining table.

She had not felt at all excited at the prospect of sitting with Lord Radford and his mother, but given that Lord Radford had insisted, she had not had any choice in the matter. Now, however, she was glad of the company, realizing that, had she not joined them, then her evening would have been spent alone in her rooms.

Not that her rooms were anything to be sniffed at, however. She had her own large bedchamber with a small dressing room to the left of it, which was more than she had ever had before. It was, for a governess' room, rather beautifully decorated with large drapes hanging either side of the window, which had immediately given her a feeling of security, recalling the man who had watched her window back in London.

"I hear you met Miss Amy earlier this afternoon,

Miss Blakely," the Dowager began, with a small smile in Elsbeth's direction. "Did you find her to be amiable?"

Thinking back to the small, blonde haired child who had looked up at her with the brightest of smiles and the bluest of eyes, Elsbeth could not help but smile. "I did," she replied, softly. "She is a beautiful little girl and I am sure we shall get along admirably."

"When do you propose to start her lessons?"

Glancing towards Lord Radford, Elsbeth hesitated for a moment before replying to the lady's question. "I would like a few days to look at the books and other resources in the schoolroom before preparing it for us both. Would that be quite all right?"

Lord Radford smiled. "More than all right, Miss Blakely. Besides, I do not think that Miss Amy will need your tutelage all day. Perhaps just in the morning, as you did with Miss Sarah?"

Elsbeth, who had been thinking much the same thing, nodded at once. "Yes, of course. I am sure she will enjoy much the same things as Miss Sarah did, and I am already looking forward to getting to know her a little better."

Looking down at her dessert, she began to eat quietly, leaving the rest of the table in silence. Nothing more was said until after their dessert was finished and the table cleared by the footmen, who Lord Radford then dismissed after requesting a tea tray for his mother and for Elsbeth.

"Should we leave you to your port?" the Dowager asked, making to rise from the table. "We can have the trays sent to the drawing room."

Lord Radford shook his head. "No, please. I think now is the time to talk about Miss Amy."

A knot formed in Elsbeth's stomach as she saw the older lady sigh and nod, looking somewhat distraught as Lord Radford sat back in his chair. What was it about Miss Amy that he wanted to say?

"As you know, Miss Blakely, Miss Amy's presence here is not well known. It has been something I have tried to keep as secret as I can."

"Even from your own mother," the Dowager muttered, drawing Elsbeth's attention. "Oh yes, Miss Blakely, I can see you are astonished to discover this but I can assure you that it is true. I was only told of her presence here less than a sennight ago and made my way here almost at once to see if it was true."

Elsbeth had a great many questions on her lips but chose not to speak any of them, seeing the distress on the lady's face and realizing that she had stepped into what appeared to be a rather difficult situation. Up until this point, she had believed that the Dowager knew about Miss Amy and had assumed that perhaps she had stayed here with Miss Amy whilst Lord Radford was in London. Now that appeared to be entirely wrong.

Lord Radford cleared his throat. "Mother, you know that I was trying to do my best by my brother."

The Dowager nodded and put her head in her hands for a moment, forcing Elsbeth to look away as a prickle of anxiety shot down her spine. This was not something she should be intruding on.

"Perhaps I should leave you be, Lord Radford," she

whispered, more worried than before. "This is a family matter and I –"

"No, stay, Miss Blakely," the Dowager interrupted before Lord Radford could even reply. "It is quite all right. I apologize for disconcerting you. It has just all been a terrible shock."

Elsbeth shut her mouth against any kind of protest and sat back her in her chair, her hands folded neatly in her lap. Thankfully, the awkward tension was broken by the footmen bringing in the tea trays, meaning that Elsbeth was able to focus on first pouring herself a cup of tea and then sipping at it carefully, whilst waiting for Lord Radford to continue.

He sighed heavily, pouring himself a glass of port.

"This is something of a sad tale, Miss Blakely, but I shall tell it nonetheless. If you are to be the child's governess then it is best you know it all."

She nodded, mutely, her mind empty as she waited for him to tell her the truth about the reason for Miss Amy's secret presence here.

"Miss Amy is the daughter of my brother, Miss Blakely."

Swallowing hard, Elsbeth tried to hide her gasp of surprise.

"She is not the daughter of his wife, however."

Her blood froze in her veins, recalling what Mrs. Simpson, the nurse, had told her. "But the children are but a few months apart, are they not?" she whispered, softly. "I don't understand."

Lord Radford gave her a small, sad smile, shrugging his shoulders. "What is there to understand, Miss

Blakely? My brother is as I was – a man used to getting what he wanted and taking his pleasures where he wanted. Unfortunately, he took that elsewhere and so the lady in question became pregnant, only a few months before his own wife did."

Elsbeth heard the Dowager draw in a shaky breath and, glancing at her, saw the paleness of her cheek. Clearly, the lady was horror-stricken.

"My brother did not care for the fact that his mistress was now with child, telling her that he would care for her by setting up a small fund and the like but, in reality, choosing not to do a thing about it." He shook his head, his lips growing thin. "In desperation, the lady came to my door with the child in her arms. I am sorry to say that she died soon afterward."

Elsbeth's hand clapped over her mouth in horror as she stared at Lord Radford.

"It was not my brother's fault that she died, nor the child's," Lord Radford continued, heavily. "A fever came upon her and there was nothing I could do. I even sent for the doctor but..." He shook his head, grief pouring into his eyes.

A brittle silence came over the room as Elsbeth continued to stare at Lord Radford, almost praying that it was not true. It was not as if she found the idea of an illegitimate child to be disturbing in any way, given that she was, most likely, one herself, but the fact that a gentleman would treat his own child with such disinterest tore at her soul.

Perhaps it was because she knew what it felt like to be so disregarded.

"You understand, I think, how that must feel," the Dowager murmured, her voice quiet. "I can see it in your eyes."

Dropping her hands back to her lap, Elsbeth gave a short, jerky nod.

"Then at least I can be assured that you will have sympathy for Miss Amy," the Dowager continued, softly. "That, at least, is a relief."

"Miss Blakely is nothing but kindness, Mother," Lord Radford added, with a slight curl of his lip. "You need not worry in that regard. Rather, you might concern yourself with how poorly your son has treated his child."

Tension grew between them as Elsbeth watched, seeing the way Lord Radford was growing angry, only for the Dowager to sigh heavily and shake her head, her shoulders slumping.

"You know why he had to do so," she muttered, looking away from Lord Radford. "I understand that, at least."

Lord Radford looked for a moment as though he were about to retort something but then chose not to, turning his gaze back towards Elsbeth.

"My brother chose to ignore the child since his own wife was expecting. He did not pretend that she was not his when I spoke to him about it but begged me to keep her presence here secret. Because I forced him into it, he is paying for her upkeep and has already set up a small inheritance for her – all unbeknownst to his wife, of course. In time, when she is grown, I will find her a good situation with a good and honest man for her husband. However, she will be known only as my ward and can never know the truth about her parentage. That must be kept quiet."

Elsbeth shook her head, a coursing anger burning through her veins. "Why must it be kept silent, Lord Radford? The child has done nothing wrong by merely existing, and yet here she is to be set aside, as though she is the one at fault, never told anything about her past and expected to accept the silence without question!"

"You do not understand, Miss Blakely," the Dowager interrupted, quietly. "My second son, the Honorable Cecil Preston, married well above his station. He was rather poor at the time, having hidden his debts and the like very well until after his marriage. I believe the lady he married thought them to be deeply in love and it was this that managed to convince Lady Beatrice's father to permit the marriage. Now, you understand, my son lives on his wife's wealth, with a great many allowances from her father. This was on the condition that he remain true and faithful."

"And so to tell society at large about Miss Amy would be to push my brother from his home and, potentially, his child and any future children from any wealth and happiness that might be theirs," Lord Radford continued, with a heavy sigh. "It is perhaps a little selfish of my brother to say such a thing, but I myself could not allow Miss Sarah to be faced with a future of difficulty over my brother's indiscretion. I thought that this would be the best for them both. I can provide for Miss Amy and ensure that she has a happy and contented life here, with a future that is secure and certain. And Miss Sarah will have much the same."

Elsbeth wanted to argue, wanted to protest, but the quiet voice within her prevented her from doing so. She could see that Lord Radford *was* doing his best for Miss Amy, yet her anger was burning over the unfairness of it all. It was as though she and Miss Amy were one and the same, even though she had no family nearby.

"And what will Miss Amy know of you?" she asked, her voice shaking a little. "Will she ever know that you are her uncle? Or will that be kept from her too?"

Lord Radford looked at her for a long time, his face devoid of expression. There was a pain in his eyes that he was trying to hide from her, as though he was attempting to be practical but struggling to contain his emotions.

"For the time being, she knows me as 'Radford' and I have not thought about anything more," he said, heavily. "She is happy and content, knowing that she is cared for and loved. Is that not enough?"

"I confess that I did not know what to say to her when I was introduced earlier today," the Dowager whispered, her face ravaged with pain. "She is my own flesh and blood, Radford, but can she ever know the connection she has with us?"

Pushing herself up from her chair, Elsbeth rose to her feet, feeling a sudden urge to be alone with her thoughts.

"Thank you, Lord Radford, but I think I will retire now," she said, picking up her tea tray and making for the door. "Clearly there are things that you need to discuss privately, and I will intrude no longer."

Lord Radford got to his feet also, coming after her. "Miss Blakely, might you...."

"Please, Lord Radford, do not trouble yourself," she

said hastily, managing to maneuver the door open before he could reach her. "Thank you for all you have given me and all you have shared with me. I confess that I am tired and need to retire soon. Good evening to you both. Thank you."

The door opened just enough for her to slip through and, with a breath of relief, Elsbeth began to make her way along the hallway and back towards the staircase, glad to be away from Lord Radford and the Dowager. It was not that she was angry with him – and she certainly had no right to be regardless, but the truth was that she was struggling with what she had heard.

Miss Amy was just as she had been, albeit in better circumstances than the Smithfield House for Girls, but the pain and the confusion she felt over not knowing her own parentage continued to grow in her regardless, along with the knowledge that one day, Miss Amy would feel the same as she. That she too would grow up without any awareness of where she had come from and with the expectation that she should appreciate what she had been given and what was offered to her. Her life would be one of mystery and confusion, questions dogging at her mind no matter how happy she became.

Her heart broke for the child, so happy and delighted in her childhood, knowing that what was waiting for her would blight that happiness entirely. Shaking her head, Elsbeth felt hot tears prick at her eyes as she stepped into her bedchamber, setting the tea tray down on the table by the small fire in the grate.

Swallowing her tears, Elsbeth turned to the door to lock it – only to see Lord Radford framed in the doorway.

"Miss Blakely," he said, his breathing ragged as though he had rushed to catch her. "I could not let you go, not when I knew you were upset over what had been said."

"I have no right to be upset," she replied resolutely, even though her heart was crying out in pain and her blood roaring in her ears. "She is your ward, Lord Radford. I am merely a servant in your employ."

He stepped forward and caught her hand in his, warmth seeping into his skin and sending vibrations up her arm. "You see yourself in her, do you not?"

The tears she thought she had banished rose once more, bursting from her eyes without warning.

"My dear Miss Blakely," Lord Radford whispered, before stepping closer and drawing her into his arms, holding her close.

Elsbeth shuddered violently, her trembling growing all the worse as Lord Radford simply stood there and held her in his arms, feeling herself grow weaker with every moment that passed. She knew he should not be doing this and that she ought not to be allowing it, but nevertheless, she continued to remain just as she was. Her head was resting on his shoulder, his arms encircling her waist and his breath dancing across her cheek.

And then, without a word, he was gone.

CHAPTER TWELVE

"Thank you," Andrew murmured as the butler handed him a sheaf of letters. "Some coffee would not go amiss either."

The butler's lips quirked as he turned away back towards the door. "But of course, my lord," he replied. "At once."

Andrew could not help but grin, aware that the butler knew of his reluctance to work through his correspondence. It had never been something he particularly enjoyed, and even though Miss Blakely's presence in his house had given him more satisfaction than ever before, he still could not turn to his correspondence with anything other than irritation.

Breaking the first seal, Andrew scanned the few short lines, reading the invitation to a house party only a short distance away from his own estate. Lord Turnbridge was well known to throw wonderful occasions and this, Andrew was sure, would be like no other.

And yet, he had no desire to go.

Getting up from his chair, Andrew made his way to the study window, his mind filled with the same person it had been caught up with these last weeks.

Miss Elsbeth Blakely.

When he had first seen her, back at the Smithfield House for Girls, he'd found her to be an intriguing beauty, with mousy brown curls escaping to blossom around her temples and such a beauty in her eyes that he had been unable to look away. A half smile caught his lips as he recalled how frosty she had been towards him, how determined she had been to ignore him – and how unwilling he had been to forget her.

It was more than just her physical beauty that tore at his heart now. He had realized that her heart and soul held just as much loveliness as her eyes and that he had come to value her honesty, her steadfastness, her determination and her compassion. Miss Blakely had become his guiding light, his beacon of hope – and he could not let her go.

Over the last fortnight, they had talked in depth about Miss Amy and about his brother's decision to completely ignore the child. He had seen her hurt, seen her pain and wanted to soothe it, aware that she saw herself in Miss Amy's shoes. It was to be expected, he supposed since they came from very similar backgrounds. Miss Amy, however, did have a family of her own surrounding her, whereas Miss Blakely had no one to call her kin. She had challenged him when it came to Miss Amy's knowledge of who he was to her, for even though the child now called him 'Radford' there would soon come a time where questions began to form in her mind, where she simply *had* to know who Andrew really was to her. He had not yet come up with a decent solution, aware that if he told her the truth that he was her uncle, she would easily surmise who her father was – and might presume that she had a mother also. It would be difficult to explain, but Andrew had seen the pain in Miss Blakely's eyes as she'd spoken of never knowing the truth about where she had come from and had known in his heart that he could not do the same thing to Miss Amy.

He had not yet fully decided what to do, but he knew in his heart that he would not allow the child to grow up with no knowledge of who she really was or where she had come from. He could still remember the smile of relief on Miss Blakely's face as he'd promised to do just that, his own heart filling as she'd done so. There was so much about her that drew him to her, so much he could not pretend did not affect him.

Miss Blakely was becoming everything to him.

Looking out at the gardens below, Andrew smiled to himself on seeing Miss Blakely and Miss Amy playing in the gardens. Miss Blakely was currently hiding behind a tree, although very plainly still in sight, whilst Miss Amy was giggling and running towards her, her face wreathed in smiles.

Miss Blakely was bringing out the best in Miss Amy, just as she had brought out the best in him.

For a second, a vision of Miss Blakely surrounded by children flashed into his mind. Her children. His children. The ones they'd brought into this world together.

The thought took his breath away and he stepped back from the window, his body alive with the idea.

Andrew found he had never wanted something so strongly in his life, realizing that the depths of feeling he had for Miss Blakely went far beyond a simple appreciation or a small fondness.

It had to be more than that. It had to be his first taste of love.

His stomach churned wildly, and his legs wobbled just a little as he went to sit back down at his desk. Love? He had never thought in all his life that he would feel such an emotion as that, having once laughed at the very idea and considered it to be nothing more than romantic nonsense, designed to make a man weak.

Yet now he welcomed it, even if he was not quite sure what to do with the emotion. It was all-consuming, devouring his soul entirely, and bringing with it such a depth of feeling that he was quite at a loss as to what to do next. Should he find Miss Blakely and confess all, in the hope that she might feel something akin to what he did? Or should he simply allow it to linger, allow it to grow until he was unable to keep silent? Putting his head in his hands, Andrew let out a long breath as his eyes looked down, unseeingly, at the letters on the table. He had very little idea as to what Miss Blakely might feel for him, even though he knew that she was, at the very least, enjoying his company and conversation as of late. They had spent hours talking and laughing and Andrew had found himself growing eager to spend more time with Miss Blakely; likewise, she did not seem disinclined towards spending time in his company either. That had to bring a spark of hope to his soul, could it not? Even his mother was taking to

Miss Blakely, which he had not been certain would occur.

Shaking his head to himself, Andrew sat back in his chair and reached for his other two letters, trying to put all thoughts of Miss Blakely to the back of his mind. The first of the two letters appeared to be from his brother and, with a small snort, Andrew deliberately set that one aside. Most likely, it would be yet more explanations as to why he had told their mother about Miss Amy, and more begging that Andrew continue on as he had done before. Andrew had no intention of treating Miss Amy any differently – in fact, Miss Blakely had encouraged him to show more interest and more care in the girl, which he had found himself willing to do – but there was no need to reply to another one of his brother's begging letters. Cecil thought of nothing and no-one but himself and it was not something Andrew wanted to encourage, even though it had never irritated him before.

"That is most likely because I was like him," he muttered aloud, picking up the second letter and turning it over.

Seeing that it was from his steward back in London and feeling a curl of excitement and trepidation in his belly, Andrew broke the seal at once and unfolded his letter. His steward had written a rather long letter and Andrew read it eagerly.

'*My Lord Radford,*' it began. '*I have made an extensive search and discovered that the Duke of Bartonshire has never once been to the Smithfield House for Girls. However, the Duke of Broadshore has recently traveled to the Smithfield House for Girls in search of one Elsbeth*

Blakely. Miss Skelton has done all she can to assist the duke and I believe the Duke to be soon coming to your estate in search of the girl. He was, I believe, taken ill in London and has been forced to wait there for some time until he recovers.'

Andrew drew in a long, steadying breath, aware that he was struggling to take in what he was reading.

'The Duke claims that Miss Blakely is his kin and, for whatever reason, is desperate to have her return with him and claim her place. If there is any more you need from me, please inform me as soon as you can and I shall continue my search at once. I am, as always, your humble servant.'

His stomach tightened painfully, his breath being pulled from his body as he stared down at the letter, slowly coming to the realization that Miss Blakely might be, in fact, related to a duke. She might be higher in society than he, might be more than he could ever be – and yet here she was, governess to his niece.

Swallowing the ache in his throat, Andrew tried to think clearly as the letter fluttered onto the table. He knew he would have to share this with Miss Blakely, but a sudden fear gripped him – a fear that she would, then, have to leave him. Leave his side and his house for good. He could not think of anything worse.

Can you really pretend this letter does not exist?

It was the same conundrum as before. To pretend that he had not received the letter would only prolong his happy situation for a short time, for the Duke would soon appear at his door. Miss Blakely had to be prepared, to know what it was that might be said, that might be revealed to her.

And he would have to tell her the truth about what he felt.

He could not pretend that there was nothing to hold her here, nothing that drove him to beg her to remain. He would have to tell her everything and not hold a single truth back. It was all still so fresh and so new to him that he could barely breathe, his lungs refusing to fill with air as he thought of speaking to her so plainly. And yet Andrew knew that it had to be done.

The dinner gong rang and Andrew looked up, startled to see just how much time had passed. Had he really been sitting at his desk for hours, his mind going over and over what his heart had finally revealed to him?

"This evening," he muttered to himself, folding up the letter and putting it in his pocket. "I shall have to talk to her this evening."

He didn't think he'd ever been more nervous in his life.

CHAPTER THIRTEEN

Elsbeth laughed as the Dowager threw down her cards, clearly frustrated with her lack of luck this time around. They had been playing cards for over an hour and, whilst the Dowager was not having the best of luck, Lord Radford appeared to be so terribly distracted that he was barely aware of when it was his turn to play.

The Dowager muttered something dark under her breath as it became Elsbeth's turn, and so play continued. Elsbeth had come to enjoy these evenings over the last two weeks, finding herself eagerly anticipating the time she would have with Lord Radford and the Dowager, both of whom were wonderful conversationalists. She felt almost a part of the family, as ridiculous a notion as that was, but it was simply due to the fact that Lord Radford had chosen not to treat her as a governess ought to be treated. Instead, for the first time in her life she was being treated as an equal. The respect and the consideration he had shown her proved, time and again, that he was not the man she had first known back at the Smithfield House for Girls. There had been a genuine and long-lasting change to his character, and it was something that Elsbeth found herself appreciating over and over again.

In fact, there was more than appreciation there. She knew that without a doubt but would not allow herself to consider what she felt, would not permit her mouth to give voice to her thoughts. That would be foolishness indeed, especially when Lord Radford had been nothing more than kind to her. He was still her employer and she was still only here until she reached the age of twenty-one, when she could finally be free.

How strange it was to consider that the dream of freedom, of a life lived just as she pleased, no longer drove her with such determination any longer. It brought her pain to think of leaving Lord Radford's home, of leaving Miss Amy and continuing on her own merry way, as her attachment to the place grew with every passing day. She did not *want* to leave Lord Radford, did not want to leave Miss Amy. Her freedom did not hold out the same joy and happiness that it once had.

"I'm afraid, Miss Blakely, that I must retire," the Dowager said, grandly, rising from her chair. "The cards are not in my favor this evening and it is growing rather late."

Elsbeth smiled and stood up as well. "But of course, Lady Radford. Thank you."

The lady smiled and then narrowed her eyes a little as she looked at Lord Radford. "And are you retiring too, Radford?"

Aware that there would be some impropriety should

the two of them remain alone, Elsbeth cleared her throat, feeling her cheeks burn. "I shall retire also, Lady Radford. Of course."

"No."

Startled, Elsbeth looked down to see Lord Radford sitting in his chair, his brows furrowed and eyes dark. She was astonished to see such a changed expression on his face, not quite certain why he now appeared to be so frustrated.

"No, Radford?" his mother asked, gently, her voice holding a hint of warning. "After all, it is –"

"Mother, I must speak to Miss Blakely alone. Some news has come from London and I must share it with her."

Elsbeth sank back down into her chair at his words, her eyes wide and her hands now fumbling to grasp the arms of the chair as a sudden weakness washed over her.

"News from London?" the Dowager asked softly, all warning gone from her voice. "I see. Then, I shall bid you both goodnight. I do hope all is well, Miss Blakely."

Elsbeth tried to nod, tried to speak, but found that both her voice and her limbs refused to work. The Dowager pressed her shoulder for a moment and then was gone, the sound of the door closing behind her making Elsbeth jump.

"Miss Blakely, are you quite all right?"

Lord Radford's voice was tender, his eyes gentle as he reached for her hand, untwining it gently from the other and holding it tightly. Her hand felt like a block of ice, his warm one slowly beginning to thaw it out.

"You look terrified, but I assure you that it is not as

bad as you might think," Lord Radford continued softly. "The letter from my steward states that the Duke of Broadshore has come in search of you. He believes you to be his family."

A few ragged gasps escaped her as Elsbeth clung to Lord Radford's hand, trying desperately to hold onto the only thing that would keep her steady.

"My steward also believes him to be coming here," Lord Radford continued, a little more quietly. "I think he intends to take you with him."

Elsbeth shook her head, her mouth working silently. The thought of leaving here to go with a man she had never met did not sit well with her. In fact, it downright terrified her.

"I do not want you to be overwhelmed but there is more that I have to say," Lord Radford said softly, sitting a little further forward in his chair so that he might look into her eyes. "Tell me what you are thinking, Miss Blakely. I can see that this is a great shock to you."

She could barely think, trying to take in the news that, supposedly, she was related to a duke. She could not imagine why he would want to come to her now, could not understand why the Duke of Broadshore would be so eager to come after her.

"But why?" she managed to say, her eyes searching Lord Radford's as though he might be able to give him an answer. "I don't understand."

Lord Radford sighed and shook his head. "I cannot answer you, Miss Blakely. Even if you are his family, you cannot inherit."

That did not matter to her. "I have a fortune waiting

for me," she whispered, putting her other hand on top of their joined ones. "I don't think I've ever told you. Once I am twenty-one, provided I remain unmarried, I shall have a fortune of my own. I will no longer need to rely on anyone."

She saw the light leave his expression, a hope in his eyes dimming and her own heart wrenched.

"That was once all that I cared about," she continued, not wanting him to think that she was desperate to leave his side. "But now I find that it no longer holds the same power it once had."

Lord Radford's mouth opened and then closed again, the question he was about to ask remaining unspoken. Elsbeth found herself looking deeply into his eyes, feeling as though he was the steadying anchor she needed, the calm eye in the storm that surrounded her.

"I do not want to be taken from this place," she whispered, feeling the way his fingers began to intertwine with her own. "This Duke, whomever he may be, has no right to force me, does he?"

The look in Lord Radford's eyes did not bring her much hope.

"I cannot say, Miss Blakely," he said, softly. "I cannot be certain about what the Duke of Broadshore wants but what I will say is that a Duke's wishes are not often easily ignored."

Fear raced up her spine, making her shiver all over. Closing her eyes, Elsbeth felt tears flood her eyes, the urge to throw herself into Lord Radford's arms and beg him to keep her safe filling her.

"But, Miss Blakely, I have to remind you that you

have always wanted to know where you have come from," Lord Radford continued, softly. "Perhaps this is the answer to your prayers and, mayhap, it should be welcomed."

That was true, she had to admit, but still, the cloying fear began to wrap itself around her throat. Shuddering violently, she shook her head, keeping her eyes shut.

"No, Lord Radford, not if he is to demand that I do as he asks, just as so many people have done before." She had not meant her words to sting but felt his hands tighten as he jerked just a little, clearly rebuked. He began to sit back, only for her to open her eyes and hold onto his hands tightly with both of her own, looking into his face with such desperation that she knew he could not help but respond.

He did not sit back and drop her hands but remained as he was, still close to her. Elsbeth let out a small sigh of relief, feeling the warm tears trickling down her cheek and knowing that she could not stop them.

"Miss Blakely, the Duke may very well reveal more to you about your family and your heritage that perhaps you have ever known," he said quietly, his eyes searching hers. "But I will not pretend that I do not think it likely that he will take you away from this place. For whatever reason, he has been looking for you and only an illness has prevented him from following after you."

She swallowed hard, remembering the man who was watching her outside the window. "Do you think that the man watching me was from the Duke?"

He shrugged. "Or Miss Skelton. Whoever it was, they want you reunited with the Duke."

That should please her, she knew, but it brought her nothing but fear. Fear that this Duke, for whatever reason, would take her away from the only place that had ever really begun to feel like home.

"I do not want to be parted from you."

The words slipped from her mouth before she could stop them, the truth ringing out between the two of them. She saw Lord Radford's eyes widen, saw the astonishment in his eyes, and knew that she had taken him completely by surprise. She had not meant to be so honest, but it had come from a place deep within herself and now it could not be unsaid. Fearing that Lord Radford would turn away from her, she closed her eyes and tried to think of something to say, something to explain what she meant – only for something soft to brush her lips.

Jumping back in surprise, Elsbeth opened her eyes to see Lord Radford's face close to hers, his eyes looking into her own.

It had been his lips. His lips on hers.

She was devoid of breath, her chest bursting with such a swell of emotion that she thought she might fracture right there in front of him.

"Miss Blakely," he whispered, letting go of her hands and running his fingers down her cheek with the utmost gentleness. "I do not want to be parted from you either."

Not for a moment did she think that he meant to have his way with her, only to discard her when he grew tired of her. She knew he was not that man any longer, for she had seen the compassion and the love within his heart for others slowly begin to grow. That man who had grabbed at her, who had done all he could to try and bring her under his spell was no longer the same man in front of her - and from the look in his eyes, she could tell that he was somewhat fearful as to what her reaction might be.

"Lord Radford, I..." she could not think of anything to say, her eyes flickering to his lips and back up to his eyes. Her heart burst open, letting the feelings and emotions she had been burying for so long spill out all at once.

It was overwhelming.

Without knowing what she was doing, Elsbeth let her arms drift up around his neck, his hair brushing the backs of her fingers. He was so close, so near to her, and Elsbeth felt her affection for him begin to grow and burn into something more. She had no idea what this meant or what would become of her should she continue along this path, but it was not something she could turn from.

His head lowered and she accepted his kiss eagerly, her heart beginning to race as he held her close. There was no urgency in his lips, no pushing her onwards, just a gentle tenderness that told her she was safe in his arms.

"Miss Blakely," Lord Radford whispered, his breathing a little ragged as he broke their kiss. "What I wanted to say to you, I will say now. I feel a great deal for you, Miss Blakely, more than I have ever felt before. I believe myself to be in love with you, although I have been too confused to see it for what it was until this very afternoon. I have been afraid that you would turn from me if I spoke to you of what I felt, afraid that I would lose you from my life. I do not want you to be a governess. I do not want you to leave my house. I do not want to be parted from you. Say that you will stay, Miss Blakely. Say that you will be my wife."

It was such a swift and startling revelation that, for a moment, Elsbeth could not speak. And yet, as she looked into his eyes, she saw the worry there, the fear that she would refuse him warring with the hope that she would agree.

She did not have to consider her answer. Lord Radford had become more to her than she had wanted to admit until now, until this very moment when she'd been forced to look into her heart and discover the true depth of her feelings. He would remain by her side, even if a thousand dukes came to claim her. With him, she was safe and secure, within his house she had found a home.

"I will," she whispered, before leaning in to touch her lips to his once more.

CHAPTER FOURTEEN

Thankfully for Andrew, his mother took the news of his engagement rather well, particularly when he mentioned that it appeared that Miss Blakely was somehow related to the duke. She declared that Miss Blakely was an excellent young lady and was clearly very good for Andrew, deciding that their marriage could go ahead without any protest from her.

Andrew himself found an excitement deep within him that was growing steadily, the arrangements for their wedding being put in place within hours of his engagement to Miss Blakely. It was very strange to have the governess still working with Miss Amy within his home when she would soon be his wife, and so Andrew determined that she should no longer be in such a role, realizing that he would soon have to find another governess for Miss Amy.

"Miss Blakely?"

Walking into the schoolroom, he saw her look up at him, the room empty except for her presence. Her eyes lit up as he walked into the room, a smile on her face as a rosy blush hit her cheeks.

He smiled back at her in return, taking her hand and lifting it to his mouth. "You are more beautiful than ever, Miss Blakely."

Her smile dazzled him. "Thank you, Radford. I think, since we are engaged, you are permitted to call me Elsbeth now."

"Elsbeth." It felt good to be able to call her by her Christian name, making him all the more aware of the intimacy growing steadily between them. How much clearer everything was today, now that their future together was secured! He had no doubt that the love he had in his heart would continue to grow, their life together as one of nothing more than sheer happiness and contentment. He kissed her hand again before dropping it, slipping one arm around her waist and pulling her a little closer to him. "Elsbeth, I have decided that you ought not to be Miss Amy's governess any longer. Nor, of course, should you be living in the governess' quarters. I intend to have your things moved to one of the bedchambers near to my mother's, although after we wed, you shall be in the room adjoining my own." He chuckled at her slightly astonished expression. "I would not have you there now, of course, for propriety's sake – although I think we have rather dashed propriety and expectation to the ground of late!"

To his surprise, Elsbeth did not smile.

"I do not want to be separated from Miss Amy," she replied, slowly. "I will continue to be her governess, Radford."

His smile faded.

"Not that I will not have my things moved, of course, which is very kind of you, but I cannot have my time with Miss Amy brought to such a hurried end – especially not when you have not yet secured another governess for her."

His gaze softened as he took in the worry in her expression, the clouding in her eyes. "You care for Miss Amy a great deal, do you not?"

She nodded slowly. "I do."

"And I should not have presumed that you would be as willing as I to drop your position here," he continued, realizing what he had done. "I should have guessed that you would stubbornly refuse to agree regardless."

He saw her eyes flare, her mouth open to protest against what he had said, only for a chuckle to escape him as she looked back at him in astonishment. Realizing that he was teasing her, Elsbeth slowly began to smile, looking away from him in slight embarrassment.

"You can be with Miss Amy for as long as you like, my love," Andrew promised, brushing his fingers down her soft cheek. "And then when the new governess arrives, you shall still spend time with her every day. I know she loves you and that you care for her deeply. I should not have expected you to simply step away from her merely because we are engaged."

Her eyes lit with happiness. "Thank you, Radford, for understanding."

"Although I will have to beg you to permit me to call the seamstress," he said, grinning. "You shall have to have a trousseau, my dear, and I will not spare any expense in that regard. Can you at least be prevailed upon to have your measurements taken so that you might order some new gowns?"

Her smile grew. "Of course, Radford. You are very kind."

Lifting her chin gently, Andrew shook his head. "Only because you have made me so, my love. I can take no credit for any of this."

A small sigh escaped her as he pressed his lips to hers, feeling her answering passion in the way she pressed her hands up against his chest, the softening of her body against his. Andrew could not recall a time that he had ever been happier.

A sharp knock on the door startled him, forcing them apart. Taking a couple of steps away from her and waiting until Elsbeth herself had sat down at her desk, he called for them to enter – only to see his butler appear, looking rather harassed.

"My lord, we have been looking all over the estate for you. Your mother is in something of a state. The Duke of Broadshore has arrived unexpectedly and is demanding to see Miss Blakely."

The bottom fell out of his world, draining away the happiness and delight he had felt only a few moments ago.

"When did he arrive?" he asked, aware of Elsbeth's gasp of surprise.

"Fifteen minutes ago, my lord. I have put him in the drawing room and the Dowager Radford sent me to search for you. I do not believe the Duke to be in the best of spirits."

"Thank you. We will be along shortly. Meanwhile, please send tea trays and the like, to refresh the Duke."

He looked over at Elsbeth and saw the way she trembled, her fingers clinging to the side of the desk.

"We must go and greet him," he said gently, coming over to her. "I will introduce you as my betrothed so that the Duke has no doubt that your place is here. I will not allow him to scare you into doing what he wishes, Elsbeth. Perhaps, after all this, he may turn out to be a kind gentleman whose only wish has been to find you and reacquaint you with your family."

He did not believe what he said at all, aware that the letter from Miss Skelton and the exchange his friend had heard between the Duke and Miss Skelton gave a very different picture of the Duke of Broadshore, but he was doing all he could to reassure Elsbeth, who was the very picture of fear.

She took his proffered arm and rose from where she sat, her eyes fixed on his.

"I will not leave you," he promised, as they made their way from the room. "Unless, of course, you do not wish to be introduced? You can listen from another room if you prefer."

Halting in the middle of the hallway, Elsbeth looked up at him. "What do you mean?"

Shrugging, he gave her a small smile. "There is a small adjoining door in the drawing room that leads to the music room. If it was to be ajar, then I am certain you could hear everything."

He waited for her to make her decision, seeing the way she considered what he had said before lifting her shoulders, drawing in a deep breath and fixing her gaze straight ahead.

"No," she said firmly, with more strength than he had expected. "No, I will not shirk from this. I have wanted to know about my family for years and I will not allow fear to hold me back. I am your betrothed and not even a Duke can prevail upon me to change my mind."

"And you are of age now to make up your own mind," Andrew replied, a sense of pride filling him as he took her in. "You are a strong, determined young woman, Elsbeth. Just remember how you fought against me!"

That, at least, brought a small smile to her face and, after a moment or two, she began to walk once more, her expression set to one of sheer determination.

Walking into the drawing room, Andrew's gaze was caught by a tall, spindly looking gentleman with a long grey beard and thick, bushy eyebrows that seemed to be in a permanent frown. He did not rise from his chair but rather looked at Andrew and Elsbeth with something like disdain, his lip curling slightly.

Andrew felt his anger begin to rise, aware that his mother also had a look of similar irritation on her face.

"The Duke of Broadshore, Radford," his mother said, getting to her feet and taking Elsbeth's arm so as to draw her to sit by her side. Andrew was relieved to see Elsbeth's hand being looped through his mother's arm, seeing the protectiveness rise in the Dowager. Clearly, she did not like the Duke of Broadshore.

"Your grace, this is my son, Viscount Radford. And this is Miss Blakely."

"How do you do, your grace?" Andrew murmured, aware that the Duke's attention was not on him but rather fixed on Elsbeth. "May I also say that Miss Blakely is my betrothed. We are to marry within a fortnight."

The Duke's sharp, beady eyes flicked to Andrew for a moment before landing on Elsbeth again.

"There will be no marriage," he said, his voice low and thin, his lips flattening as he saw Elsbeth's astonished expression. "I have other plans for my granddaughter."

Hearing Elsbeth's gasp of surprise, Andrew forced himself not to go to her, choosing to remain standing. "Miss Blakely is your granddaughter?"

"She is."

"And how long have you known?"

Andrew turned to see Elsbeth gazing back at the older gentleman with such firmness in her gaze that a burst of pride soared through him. She was not about to quiver and shake beneath the man's gaze, nor accept that what he said was true. She was finding the strength within herself to stand up against this man's stern words.

The Duke sniffed. "I have always known. Who do you think sends money towards your education?"

Elsbeth drew in a breath, and Andrew fought the urge to put one hand on her shoulder. He had to allow her to do this herself. He could see the suffering in her expression, the way she had to take a moment to keep her composure steady so that she did not shrink in front of this man.

"And I was never allowed to know of your existence?"

Her voice was clear and steady and the Duke returned her gaze with nothing more than indifference. Andrew wanted to plant the man a facer, despite his age and status, more than aware that he cared not a jot for Elsbeth.

"I did not think it necessary for you to know anything about your family," the Duke replied, in a haughty voice. "After all, you were unwanted, and I had very little intention of ever revealing your existence to the world."

Elsbeth swallowed hard. Her hands were clenched in her lap, with the Dowager's hand now settled on her shoulder. She was doing all she could to be strong, to continue to force herself not to give in to tears or the like, determined not to show any kind of emotion towards this man that sat there so arrogantly on the edge of Andrew's sofa.

"And why, might I ask, are you so eager to pursue an acquaintance with me now?"

All eyes turned towards the Duke who, without even breaking into a smile, gave a small shrug. "It has become necessary."

"Why?"

A long sigh escaped him. "I had a son, and one I chose to adopt as my own. One from my first marriage, the other from my second." He leaned back in his chair, not even a hint of emotion in his words. "My first wife died in childbirth, but the child – my heir – survived. My second wife was a widow with, at the time, a very young son who I chose to adopt as my own, although she recently also passed away. I never for one moment thought that this adopted son would end up becoming the heir to the Dukedom." Giving a slight sniff, the Duke paused for a moment, his gaze still fixed on Elsbeth. "My first son was foolish indeed, managing to die without doing his duty. He did not produce an heir but did, in fact, produce an illegitimate child. You."

Andrew's hands curled into fists as Elsbeth lifted her chin, no shame in her eyes. She was not about to take any kind of blame for being illegitimate, as though such a thing was her fault. However, the Duke appeared to be blaming Elsbeth entirely, as though her very existence was the reason for his ire.

"So therefore, this man you call your son – whose name I do not yet know – put me into the Smithfield Home for Girls."

The Duke's face tightened into a sneering smile. "Well, given that my sister-in-law, the pious Miss Skelton, runs the place, I did not have much of a choice."

Andrew stared at the Duke, aware of the gasp of surprise that had come from both his and Elsbeth's lips. "Miss Skelton is your sister in law?"

The Duke's sneer grew. "Yes. Reverted to her Christian name when my stupid brother decided to depart from this earth at a rather young age and leave her with nothing but a decent fortune. I believe she blamed the death of her husband on herself and thought to run the House for Girls as a way of making up for her sins."

"Her sins?" Elsbeth asked, weakly. "What sins?"

Shrugging, the Duke appeared completely nonchalant. "I am not altogether sure, but needless to say my brother's death was from his insistence on drinking too much and spending too much time away from his wife's bed." He sniffed again, his gaze darting away for a moment. "Someone pulled him out of the Thames and within a fortnight, Miss Skelton was in the House for Girls as the new owner. Not that I particularly cared at the time, but she certainly did prove useful when it came to finding you a place, Miss Blakely."

Andrew could not contain himself any longer. "And I presume 'Miss Blakely' is not her real name?"

"Oh, it is real enough!" the Duke replied, throwing him a hard look. "Blakely is an old family name and it was put there on her birth certificate. Not likely that anyone would be able to trace her back to our family, however, especially since Miss Skelton assured me that she would keep all that under lock and key."

Elsbeth shook her head. "Miss Skelton always disliked me."

"Of course, she did," the Duke replied, disparagingly. "You are illegitimate. An unwanted child. A mistake. A shame to our family that must be hidden. Miss Skelton, being as pious as she was, had nothing but dislike for you. She only put up with you because she was generously reimbursed for the trouble."

"And why ensure that I had a good living?" Elsbeth asked, her voice now growing hard as a flare of anger burned in her eyes. "Why give me a good dowry? Why permit me to have the dowry as my fortune if I did not marry?"

Something like irritation flashed across the Duke's face. "You were never meant to learn of that part," he replied, brusquely. "Miss Skelton was *meant* to ensure that you wed before the age of twenty-one but, if she was unable to find you a husband, then the fortune meant that you could make your own way in the world and she would no longer have the burden of your presence on her shoulders. I could have sent you to the poorhouse, of course, but there was always the chance that you might, somehow, discover where you came from and we could not have that. Besides," he finished, with eyes that fixed on Elsbeth's face, "I wanted to make sure that, should you ever prove useful, I would know where you were. As it is, you are to become useful to me once more. It seems those years at the House for Girls and the money spent on you have not been entirely for nothing."

Stepping forward, Andrew shook his head, his lips thin and jaw clenched. "You treat this wonderful young lady as though she were nothing more than a stain on your perfectly white gown. How dare you?!"

The Duke lifted his gaze and fixed it on Andrew's hot face, his lip curled. "That is because she *is* a stain, Viscount Radford. A stain that, unfortunately, I must now merge with the rest of the spotless white linen."

His anger bursting into life, Andrew made to step closer, only for Elsbeth to catch his hand and pull him back. Dropping his gaze to her, he saw her look up at him with anxiety in her expression, her hand holding his tightly.

"Do not," she whispered, squeezing his hand. "I have a home here now. None of this matters."

"It *will* matter, Miss Blakely, given that you are to come with me now, in order to marry."

Turning towards him, Andrew shook his head firmly. "Elsbeth is engaged to me. I will not give her up to another."

The Duke chuckled, his eyes dark. "My dear Lord Radford. Whatever makes you believe she has a choice?"

CHAPTER FIFTEEN

Elsbeth ignored the Duke entirely, even though her breath was coming quick and fast, her mind spinning with all that she had been told. She kept her gaze fixed on Radford, telling herself over and over that *he* was the one she could depend on, that *he* was the one to keep her safe and secure.

"You are to come with me this very moment, Miss Blakely," the Duke continued. "And I'd ask you to start showing me a little more respect. I am a Duke, after all. You are expected to refer to me as 'your grace', although I can see you have some rather poor examples around you."

He sniffed, again, but Elsbeth forced herself not to give him any of her attention, not until she saw Andrew draw in a long breath, some of the tension leaving his face. Then, taking in a deep breath of her own, she turned back to the Duke.

"I will not be leaving with you, *your grace,*" she replied, calmly. "I have an engagement here, I'm afraid. I am to marry Lord Radford in a few short weeks."

The older man did not so much as move.

"Whether or not you think I ought to give you any respect, I choose not to align myself with my true family," she continued, her voice calmer than she had hoped. "I have found a home here and this is where I shall remain."

A small, exasperated sigh left the Duke's mouth. "You are to marry, Elsbeth. My first son, the true heir, died by falling from his horse a year or so ago, having never produced another child within his own marriage. His wife's womb remains barren." He shook his head, showing no emotion over the loss of his only son. "Therefore, I am left with the second son – the one who is not even my own blood, to continue the family line. This I will not have." He tipped his head and sent a piercing look towards Elsbeth. "As much as I dislike it, you are my own flesh and blood and, therefore, you will wed my stepson Lord Drake, and produce the heir. He is a decent man, I suppose and has not yet wed. I have told him that I will procure his bride and so I have. He is already waiting."

Elsbeth struggled to breathe, feeling as though the walls of the house were closing in around her. Here she was again, in a position where life was being pushed at her as though she had no choice of her own. She was expected to do as she was told without any question, without any kind of thought to her own feelings on the matter.

Lord Radford's hand tightened in her own. "As Miss Blakely has made very clear, your grace, she will not be going with you. She is already spoken for and, as such, I fear you have made a wasted trip."

A harsh laugh escaped from the Duke's mouth. "Miss Skelton told me not to come after you, Miss Blakely, told me that you would be more trouble than you are worth but I'm afraid that I am not convinced. Yes, Miss Blakely, you will come. Else I will reveal that the child within this home does not belong to Lord Radford but to his brother." He chuckled again as Lord Radford's mouth dropped open. "Yes, I am fully aware of the difficulties this might cause for your brother and his family, Lord Radford. You did not think that I came here under the assumption that my granddaughter would merely agree to come with me, did you?"

A feeling of revulsion climbed up Elsbeth's throat.

"I cannot believe you would do this," she whispered, her heart aching and torn over the knowledge that this man, this cruel, selfish, disdainful man, was her own flesh and blood. "Why would you put this on them? Onto me?"

The Duke's smile lingered. "Because I expect you to do as I ask and, if you do not, then I will force you to do so. You need to learn, just as the rest of my family have done, that my word is to be obeyed."

Slowly, Elsbeth began to pull her hand away from Radford's, aware that there was nothing she could do but agree. She could not allow Miss Sarah to live a life of difficulty, simply because of Elsbeth's own selfish ambition.

"No."

Lord Radford's harsh voice caught her ears, forcing her to look up at him.

"No, your grace, Miss Blakely will not be coerced into doing anything she does not wish."

"Radford!" the Dowager exclaimed, horrified. "But the reputation! The shame!"

Lord Radford shook his head. "It is what my brother deserves, mama. He was the one to do such a shameful thing and it is his burden to bear. I will not allow Miss Amy to be used as a bargaining chip." He turned towards the Duke, his stance firm. "Your grace, do as you wish. If it comes to it, I will give my brother and his family a living, but the shame of his illegitimate child will not be used to force Elsbeth to do as you wish."

Elsbeth's heart was hammering so hard, she was certain they could all hear it. Her mind was screaming at her to say something, to *do* something, but she could not think what it was she could do.

"Radford, no," she whispered, tugging at his arm. "I cannot let this happen."

He turned to face her, his gaze steady and filled with such gravity that she could not help but shiver.

"No, Elsbeth, please," he replied, softly. "This is not to be allowed. My brother may be cut off from his father in law, but that will be the consequence of his own actions. He will have no-one to blame but himself."

"But his wife and Miss Sarah!" Elsbeth protested, her heart hurting for what they would experience. "What will become of them?"

He shook his head, a small smile on his lips. "I should have expected you to think of others before yourself, my love. His wife and my niece will be well taken care of, from my own pockets. I assure you of that. And when the time comes for my niece to wed, then the scandal will be old and forgotten, with new ones chasing the *beau monde* around town." He gave a small shrug. "Who knows? Perhaps she will wish to know her half-sister. After all, they are family."

Elsbeth did not know how to respond, both terrified and relieved in equal measure. She looked desperately into Lord Radford's eyes, her gaze begging him to change his mind but, of course, he remained steadfast.

"Then they shall have my dowry," she whispered, as he ran a gentle finger down the curve of her cheek. "If this is my doing then I shall give them my fortune."

Lord Radford smiled softly, ignoring the muttering that was now coming from the Duke. "It is not your doing, Elsbeth. You need to remember that. I shall take care of my brother and his family if it comes to it, showing care and consideration for those within my family. Just as you have taught me to do."

It was with resolve that Elsbeth then turned her gaze back to the Duke, realizing that not only was her betrothed not going to give in, but that she did not want to give in either. The Duke of Broadshore was not someone she wanted to know and certainly not someone she wished to have in her life. Nor Miss Skelton, for that matter, even though she was, somehow, related to her through marriage. It was all very confusing and yet, through it all, her trust in Lord Radford remained steadfast.

"It appears that things will go just as I had intended," she said quietly, as the Duke's eyes narrowed. "I am sorry that you came here on a wasted journey, grandfather, but

I will not be going back with you. I will not be used as a pawn in your chess game."

He slammed one fist down on his knee and started forward, his gaze hard. Gone was the indifferent demeanor, gone was the arrogant sneer. Instead, there was only fury.

"You will do as I say!"

Elsbeth got to her feet and held onto Lord Radford's hand for dear life, doing all she could to present a calm yet firm demeanor even though she was quailing inside.

"If you will excuse me, your grace, I have some things I must attend to," she replied, quietly. "I will not say it was a pleasure to meet you, for I have been sorely disappointed to know that you are my family." She took in his angry gaze, his twisted lips and furious stance as he rose to his feet but felt no guilt nor shame. The Duke of Broadshore was not a man she wanted to see again and the sooner he was gone from Lord Radford's home, the better.

"I think your time in my home has come to an end, your grace," Lord Radford added mildly, as the Dowager came to stand by Elsbeth's side. "Good day to you."

The duke could not say anything, his jaw working furiously as he tried to find a way to force Elsbeth to do as he wished. The three of them stood together as he stood there alone, united in their desire for this man to be gone.

"Good day, your grace," the Dowager said firmly, as the door was opened by the butler. "And next time, may I suggest you make an appointment?"

There was no response. Instead, with only one last furious glare in Elsbeth's direction, the Duke began to make his way towards the open door, muttering under his breath. Elsbeth maintained her strong stance, keeping her eyes fixed on him, unwilling to crack whilst he was still in the room. It was only when the butler closed the door firmly behind him that Elsbeth felt herself begin to shake, overcome by all that had occurred.

Lord Radford's arm was around her waist, helping her to sit back down, his strength supporting her as she collapsed into sobs. His voice murmured in her ear over and over again, telling her how strong she had been, how proud he was of her and just how much his love for her had grown.

He is all I need, she told herself, her tears blurring her vision as she looked up into his face. *I will be his wife. I need not think of the Duke again. That part of my life is over.*

"You did marvelously well, my dear," Lord Radford murmured, as the Dowager rang the bell for tea. "I confess myself greatly astonished at what he said. I cannot imagine how much those words must have hurt you."

His compassion and sympathy were a balm to her soul, the pain that the Duke had caused already lessening.

"I will not let him take you away, not when you are already so precious to me," he whispered, softly. "You are a priceless jewel and I cannot let you go. Not for any price."

A lump formed in her throat as she looked back at him, knowing that every word he said was true. "Thank you, Radford. I don't know what I would have done without you." She shuddered, violently. "To go with him, to marry a man I did not know simply to preserve his family line...." She shook her head, her lips quivering. "To be used just as I have been before."

He held her close, as the Dowager stepped to the window to give them a moment or so of privacy. "You need never worry about that again," he said, quietly, his lips brushing her brow. "You are to be treasured, Elsbeth. Always."

CHAPTER SIXTEEN

The following week seemed to pass with very little to concern anyone. Elsbeth spent her time being measured for new gowns, slowly choosing to don the new creations for dinner, whilst remaining in her governess' gowns during the day. To her very great delight, she received a letter from Mrs. Banks, whom she had written to almost the moment she had become engaged. Mrs. Banks was effervescent in her joy for all that had occurred in Elsbeth's life, telling her that she deserved to have such a great happiness thrust upon her. Elsbeth read the letter more than a few times before tucking it carefully away, intending to reply to Mrs. Banks again soon. Perhaps, she had mused to herself, Mrs. Banks would, one day, be able to come and live with herself and Lord Radford, perhaps as nurse to the children Elsbeth could, one day, hope to have. It was a wonderful thought and gave her a great deal of happiness.

To Elsbeth's very great relief, Miss Amy, it seemed, took the news of her governess' marriage to her Uncle Radford – as he had now told her he was – quite on the chin, seemingly neither delighted nor irritated with the idea.

She was, after all, not yet five years of age.

Elsbeth smiled to herself as she watched the girl play on the lawn, swinging idly on one of the swings she had found tied to a large tree in the center of the gardens. It was, of course, meant for Miss Amy, but Elsbeth often found herself drawn to it when the child was interested in nothing more than running around the gardens for a few minutes.

It also gave her time to think, and she had, of late, had a great deal to think about.

After the meeting with the Duke, the dowager had grown rather icy towards not only her but also her son, seemingly fraught with worry over what the Duke might do with his threats over Cecil's indiscretions. Radford, however, had remained resolute and had told Miss Amy that he was, in fact, her uncle and that she was to call the dowager 'grandmama'. The Dowager had not been given any choice in the matter but Elsbeth had, at least, seen a small smile escape from the lady when the small child had addressed her as such.

From that day, the lady had become a little warmer towards them both, seemingly accepting that Cecil's indiscretions would eventually catch up with him as it ought. She had also been bolstered by the promise that Radford and Elsbeth alike would do what they could for the family, if it came to it. As yet, no news had been heard from either Cecil or the Duke, although Elsbeth was still quite certain that the Duke would do as he had threatened. He did not seem like the kind of man to make a threat only to toss it aside.

For her part, however, she had taken what she had learned from the Duke and chosen to put it all behind her. She was, of course, deeply hurt to learn that the family she had so often dreamed of had turned out to be nothing more than arrogant and self-centered creatures, who both looked down at her and wanted to use her for their own ends, but the assurance of a brighter future with a man who loved her, a man who had changed before her very eyes, gave her more happiness than the pain she felt over the Duke's revelations. It had been difficult to hear about Miss Skelton, the news that her father was now deceased, as well as the Duke's intentions for her but, with a will, Elsbeth had put it all behind her. She did not allow her thoughts to dwell on it but rather thought of her future with Lord Radford. She thought of her trousseau slowly being put together, of her life with him and Miss Amy, of a house that would soon be hers to run. Dreams filled her mind, dreams of children and a family of her own, a home filled with nothing but love and laughter. A home devoid of everything that had caused her own childhood so much pain.

"Do be careful, Miss Amy!" she called, seeing the child almost falling to her knees as she ran, heedlessly, around the bushes that dotted the gardens. She was going to tire herself out which, given the amount of energy she had, would be rather a good thing! She laughed as the child came to a sudden stop, her eyes widening as a small, delicate butterfly landed on her arm, its wings fluttering gently.

"If you want no harm to come to the child, you will come with me now."

A harsh, angry voice muttered in her ear and, without being able to prevent it, a scream left Elsbeth's mouth – only for a dirty hand to be slapped over her mouth. Her eyes turned to see a large, burly man standing directly behind her, his smile cruel.

"Send the girl indoors."

Elsbeth looked back to see Miss Amy still standing exactly where she was, although her eyes were wide as she took in the man by Elsbeth's side. She made to get up, only for the man to clap one hand on her shoulder.

"Don't so much as move."

Swallowing her fear, Elsbeth tried to smile and beckoned Miss Amy towards her. She did not want to bring any harm to the child, knowing that she had no other choice but to do what the man said.

"Miss Amy, I think it is best if you run along inside now," she said, in as cheerful a voice as she could. "This man is to show me where the most beautiful flowers are in the gardens, and I shall bring some to you."

The girl appeared to be a little relieved, a small smile on her face although her eyes continued to dart up towards the man standing there. Elsbeth felt a coil of fear in her belly as she tried to smile, desperate for the child to hurry inside, where she would be safe.

"Off you go now," she said, patting Miss Amy's arm.

"I am sure I heard Nurse say something about having your favorite dessert this evening. Why don't you go and ask her? I will be along in a few minutes with some flowers for your table."

Miss Amy's face lit up and, with a delighted squeal, she hurried towards the front of the house, leaving Elsbeth sitting with the large gentleman still behind her.

"Very good," he grated, as something sharp touched the skin between her shoulder blades. "Now move."

Hiding a gasp, Elsbeth got to her feet and did as she was told, walking in the direction the man gestured towards. They were headed towards a large copse of trees near the end of the large gardens, where it would be very difficult for anyone in the house to see her. She didn't want to go, didn't want to leave Miss Amy or Lord Radford behind but, since she had a knife to her back, Elsbeth knew she had no other choice.

"Why are you doing this?" she asked, her voice shaking as she was hurried forward. "What do you mean to do?"

A harsh laugh shook her very core.

"You'll find out soon enough," the man chuckled, putting one hand on the small of her back to hurry her along even more. "Although I should warn you not to say no to this particular gentleman again. You'll soon learn he always gets what he wants."

Elsbeth stifled a gasp of horror, realizing that the man could only be talking about the Duke. There *was* no-one else that she'd refused recently, and apparently refusing the Duke was not something she was to be allowed to do.

"Hurry now."

Walking into the copse of trees, Elsbeth found herself staring at an old hackney, with a single horse pulling it. She was shoved unceremoniously inside, only to see the Duke of Broadshore sitting opposite her.

"Very good, Stephens," he muttered, as the man shut the door tightly. "You'll be well recompensed for this. Now take us back to the carriage."

Elsbeth could do nothing but stare at the older man, her heart sinking down to her toes. He was looking back at her with nothing but calm assurance, as though he knew full well what he had done and was almost proud of it. He had told her that he was not used to anyone refusing him and now it appeared that he would do whatever he had to in order to get his way.

"Let me go."

Her words were whispered yet fierce, her heart clamoring within her chest. Elsbeth felt her hands clench, her fingers biting into the soft skin of her palms as tears formed in her eyes as the hackney rolled forward. She was not about to give in and simply allow the Duke to get his way, even if he was her family.

"Now, now, Elsbeth, now is not the time to be demanding anything," the Duke replied, lazily. "Haven't you learned by now that I am not to be trifled with?"

Swallowing the ache in her throat and forcing her tears back, Elsbeth lifted her chin. "This is not right. I am to marry Lord Radford."

The Duke snorted in derision. "I think not. A viscount is too far below you, Elsbeth, whereas the next Duke of Broadshore is more than perfect."

"And it gets you what you want," she retorted,

angrily. "I am not to be used in such a way, your grace! I will not do this. I will not marry your stepson."

He looked back at her almost lazily, as though he had been expecting her to say such things and found her predictable.

"I am sure that, in time, you will come to see things my way," he replied, softly, one hand now gesturing to the seat beside him. "My stepson will be your husband and you will bring back the Dukedom to my family line."

Elsbeth caught her breath as she saw the pistol sitting on the seat next to the Duke. He had not left anything to chance and would use this weapon to force her to obey him. It would be either that or death.

Swallowing her tears and her anger, Elsbeth sat back in her seat and felt her strength ebb away. The hackney continued on through the gardens, until it came to a hidden entrance in the wall, making its way carefully through it. She had not even known such a path existed.

There was nothing she could do. The hackney would continue to take her further and further away from the Radford Estate, away from the man she loved, and all she could do was sit there and allow it to happen. Either that or face death. Closing her eyes, Elsbeth tried her best to build her strength, telling herself that, somehow, she would find a way out of this situation, but her pain and her helplessness increased all the more. Opposite her, she heard the Duke laugh softly, as though he were aware of her pain and somehow, in his own twisted way, saw it as a victory.

Elsbeth fought tears, refusing to let a single one fall to her cheek as the sound of the Duke's laughter rang in her ears. Fixing her mind on Lord Radford, she kept him in her thoughts as the hackney continued on, praying that somehow, Miss Amy would have found him and told him about the strange man in the garden.

It was the only flicker of hope she had left.

CHAPTER SEVENTEEN

"Miss Amy?"

"Grandmama!"

Andrew chuckled as he saw the child hurry towards the Dowager, aware that his mother was still not quite used to being referred as such. They had both come out of the drawing room together, having looked over the menus for the week, and had seen the girl come in from the gardens.

"My goodness, child, you are looking rather windswept," the Dowager commented, as the young girl beamed up at her. "Do not tell me that Miss Blakely has been allowing you to run around like a mad thing?"

Chuckling quietly at the slight smile on his mother's face, Andrew made to turn away to leave them to converse, only to come to a sudden stop as Miss Amy spoke again.

"Miss Blakely was with a man."

Slowly, Andrew turned around, seeing his mother look back at him with a sudden, sharp look.

"A man?" she asked, as Andrew came back to them. "Is that so? Where is Miss Blakely?"

The girl shrugged. "She went with the man."

Aware that there could be staff listening and trying to ignore the worry tightening in his chest, Andrew beckoned his mother back towards the drawing room.

"Come in here, Miss Amy, and you can tell me everything," the Dowager replied, in a warm tone so as not to frighten the girl. "I confess I am very interested to discover who this man might be."

Closing the door to the drawing room tightly, Andrew leaned back against it for a moment as the Dowager led Miss Amy to sit down on one of the comfortable sofas.

"Now, who is this man?" she asked softly, as soon as the girl was settled. "Had you seen him before?"

Miss Amy shook her head, a frown on her face. "I don't think so. I thought he might have been one of the gardeners."

"Why would you think that?" Andrew asked, coming towards her and bending down on his haunches to look into her eyes. "Did he say he was?"

Miss Amy paused for a moment before shaking her head. "No, but Miss Blakely said they were going to pick some flowers for the table. She said he was going to show her where the prettiest flowers in the gardens were."

"I see." Andrew tried to smile as Miss Amy looked back at him, clearly very concerned. He knew in an instant that there was something grievously wrong, although he could not quite say what it was.

"And did Miss Blakely send you inside?" the

Dowager asked softly, as he got to his feet to lean on the mantlepiece, his eyes gazing down into the flickering flames in the grate below. "Is that why you came inside on your own?"

Glancing behind him, Andrew saw Miss Amy nod, her eyes widening. Walking over to the bell, Andrew tugged it twice, aware that he would need his butler.

"She said she would be inside very soon," she said softly, her chin beginning to wobble a little. "I didn't like the man, but Miss Blakely was very insistent that I go inside. Did I do something wrong?"

Andrew turned back to face her, seeing his mother put one arm around the girl's shoulders. "Of course not," he said, gently. "I think Miss Blakely was trying to keep you safe, Miss Amy. Now, can you tell me what this man looked like?"

A bubble of frustration broke open as the girl told him about what the man looked like, for it was such a simple description that he could not exactly narrow it down. The man was, according to Miss Amy, tall with dark hair, a dirty face and terribly crooked teeth. She had never seen him before, which meant that, most likely, Andrew had never seen him before either. However, the one thing the girl *could* tell him was that, just before she'd come inside, she'd looked back over her shoulder and seen the man walking with Miss Blakely towards the other end of the gardens, towards the trees.

"Thank you, Miss Amy, you've been very helpful," he said, patting her hand. "Now, why don't you run along to find Nurse? Make sure to tell her that you're to have some cocoa; won't that taste good?"

The child's face brightened at once, still clearly unaware of exactly what had happened to Miss Blakely and, with another smile, she made her way to the door, only to be met by the butler.

"Have one of the footmen escort Miss Amy to the nurse," Andrew said firmly. "Then come back here. I have need of you."

The butler nodded at once and followed Miss Amy out of the door, leaving Andrew to let out a long breath, sink into a chair and put his head in his hands.

"What do you think has become of her, Radford?"

The Dowager's voice was tired, yet pained, making Andrew aware of just how much his mother had come to appreciate Miss Blakely.

"I think this can only be the Duke of Broadshore, Mother," he said through his hands. "There is an old, overgrown path that leads to the edge of the estate down by those trees, although it has not been used for some time. I would suspect that Miss Blakely has been forcibly removed from the premises so that the Duke might get what he wishes.

Looking up at his mother, Andrew saw her nod slowly, her eyes widening as she looked back at him.

"Then what do we do?"

He opened his mouth only to find that there was no easy answer. He wanted to tell her that they would simply go after her, only to realize that he had no idea in which direction she had gone nor where the Duke of Broadshore had headed. He could be going to his own estate, or to the estate of his stepson. Perhaps a church, or to London to fetch a special license so Miss Blakely could marry there. Andrew had little doubt as to what the Duke had planned for Miss Blakely, aware that she would somehow be forced into matrimony to the Duke's stepson.

"Andrew," his mother said softly, using his Christian name in an attempt to encourage him. "What is it you are thinking of doing? I know you will not let Miss Blakely be so easily taken from you."

"I....."

The words died on his lips as he tried his best to think of what to do, finding that he could not come up with anything in particular.

"I don't know, Mother," he admitted, lifting his face from his hands. "I must get her back, but I have no idea where I might start. If I go after her in one direction, then she might very well be traveling in the opposite direction. What do I do?"

A quiet rap came to the door as Andrew looked back helplessly at his mother, calling for the butler to enter. Out of the corner of his eye, Andrew saw the butler come in and close the door quietly behind him, standing there stoically until Andrew spoke to him.

"Miss Blakely has been taken," he said, hollowly, his fear and frustration rising with almost every word he spoke. "I do not know where she has gone. Send the footmen out to search and have riders sent to the nearby inns to discover if anyone of importance is to reside there."

The butler's eyes flared for a moment, and he nodded.

"Miss Amy saw Miss Blakely being taken to the

bottom of the gardens, so I think you might begin there," he continued, not knowing what else to do. "And if there are tracks of any kind, I want them followed for as long as possible."

"Right away, my lord," the butler said hastily, making to close the door. "Is there anything else?"

Andrew made to shake his head, only for his mother to hold up one hand.

"Have a bag made up for Lord Radford," she said, glancing back at Andrew. "Nothing too much, just something he can take with him on horseback. He is, of course, going to fetch Miss Blakely home."

The butler nodded and disappeared, leaving Andrew to look back at his mother with nothing more than sheer helplessness burning in his soul.

"How can I fetch her if I do not know where she is gone?" he asked, heavily. "Mother, I –"

"If you go one way, then I shall go the other," she interrupted, softly. "You are not in this alone, Andrew. I will do all I can to help." Reaching forward, she touched his cheek gently, her eyes soft as he looked back at her. "My son, you have become the man I have always hoped you would be, and I can see that it is due to Miss Blakely's support. I would not have her gone from this house, gone from your life. I know that she means more to you than you can say, and it is impossible not to see the love she has for you in her own heart. I have come to value her and I will not allow her to be simply taken away against her will when I know her place and her heart is here." She smiled at him gently, her eyes filled with hope that, slowly, began to pierce Andrew's heavy heart.

"I hope so, Mother," he admitted, quietly. "I feel as though I have lost her for good. I do not even know where to begin to look."

"Patience," came the steady reply. "I know that it appears as though all is lost but give your staff some time. It is difficult to remain here when she is gone from you – I understand that, of course – but patience will be your guide. Let them find a path for you to follow first. Then your chances of returning Miss Blakely here increase tenfold."

It was agony to wait. For hours, Andrew was forced to either sit or stand as his staff made a thorough search of the grounds, as still others rode off in every direction to seek news from the nearby inns. His heart went from overwhelming hope to unspoken agony over and over again, whilst, all the time, his mother simply sat with her hands in her lap, silently praying.

He could not lose Elsbeth, not now. Not when they had become so close, when they had started a life together that he could not imagine living without her. His mother was right to say that she had become more to him than he could say, for he had never known what it was to love another before with his whole heart. "My lord?"

Andrew's head jerked up as the butler opened the door, beckoning the man inside.

"What have you found?"

The butler cleared his throat and, for the first time, Andrew saw that he appeared to be rather pale.

He swallowed hard. This did not bode well.

"We found that a carriage or the like must have been in the gardens, my lord, making its way out of the small gap in the walls that is no longer used."

Andrew groaned and put his head in his hands.

"However, there has come news from one of the riders, my lord," the butler continued, his voice still grave. "One of the inns – the Winter Arms - is rather quiet – unusually so. The innkeeper was unwilling to take on any new guests but would not say why, which is rather strange given that it is so quiet."

Looking up, Andrew saw a flare of hope in his mother's eyes, hope which was reflected in his own heart.

"Another rider has returned with some items he found along the road as he rode out from the house, which he thought to bring back with him, just in case they belonged to Miss Blakely."

Andrew got to his feet, seeing the five small items on a tray that was passed to the butler by a footman still outside the door. His eyes took in the three bits of torn material, not understanding what they were until he saw the initials embroidered on one of them.

"This was her handkerchief?" he whispered, taking in the 'E.B' emblazoned on one of the corners. "And these two pieces....?" He picked up a scrap of dark grey material, seeing a small button still attached.

His mother hurried towards him in a flurry of skirts. "Oh, Radford," she breathed, taking it from him. "Is that not a cuff from her gown?"

It made sense. It was the same color as Miss Blakely's governess dresses and given that he also held the pieces of her handkerchief in his hand, it could only mean one thing.

"And this rider did not see a carriage on the road?" he asked, seeing the butler shake his head. His flare of hope began to fade as he set the pieces of material back on the tray, confused as to where he might be.

"No, he did not, but I believe he chose to return with these items rather than continue along the road in search of Miss Blakely and the carriage."

Andrew nodded slowly, his heart beginning to quicken. "I see. And does the road lead towards the inn?"

The butler paused. "It very well could do, my lord. The man who went to the inn took the shortest route, crossing through fields and the like, whereas the road would take a little more time but, from what I know of the land, would lead there eventually."

"Then I must start there," Andrew replied, catching his mother's eye and seeing her nod. "The man will need to show me the road where he found these," he continued, gesturing towards the tray. "And I intend to leave at once."

The butler nodded. "Of course, my lord. I will have your horse readied at once."

Andrew drew in a long breath and caught his mother's hands as she stepped closer, aware of the worry in her eyes.

"I pray I will find her, Mother," he whispered softly, pressing her hands. "I do not think I will be able to return without her."

She paused and nodded, her lips trembling just a little. "I am afraid of what that man will do to you, should you find her," she admitted eventually, her hands tightening on his. "You must be careful, Radford. The Duke is not a man to be crossed."

"I will not be afraid of him," Andrew replied, firmly, his jaw set. "He may be a Duke, but I will not allow him to do just as he pleases with Miss Blakely, nor with our family."

"Promise me you will be careful."

Bending to kiss her cheek, Andrew drew in a long, steadying breath against the anger and the fear churning wildly in his stomach. "Of course, I will, Mother," he promised, as quietly and as calmly as he could. "Might you ensure that Miss Amy is not distraught or upset in any way? I am sure she could do with some reassurance from you."

He saw his mother nod, aware that in sending her to speak to Miss Amy, he would be helping his mother to forget her anxiety somewhat. Miss Amy would keep his mother company as she waited for him to return, helping her not to watch the minutes or the hours pass by.

Pressing her hands again gently, Andrew walked towards the door, his shoulders set and jaw clenched. He was resolute in his determination to find Miss Blakely, even if it took him hours, days, or weeks. He would have her back in his home, back by his side, back as the love of his life. Life without her was unthinkable.

"I am coming for you, Elsbeth," he whispered to himself, as he mounted his horse, feeling it dance with anticipation. "Just hold on a little longer. I will be with you again very soon."

CHAPTER EIGHTEEN

Elsbeth stared down at her torn cuffs, wondering if Radford had found her clues that she had surreptitiously managed to throw out of the window. The Duke had not appeared to notice, his eyes closed as the hackney had continued to move forward along the road, although the pistol had been firmly held in one hand, pointed in her direction.

It had taken all her courage to tear her handkerchief into three pieces, cringing as the sound of it ripping bouncing around the hackney – but the Duke had not stirred. She had not dared throw anything more than those five pieces out of the window, realizing that she had nothing else to discard even if she'd wanted to.

She had no idea how long they'd traveled for, but eventually they'd come to a stop at some inn or other, where she'd been warned not to make a sound, a knife point pressed into her back again as they'd walked towards the inn.

And now here she was, in a small room in some

unknown inn, left in peace to eat and drink to refresh herself for what was to come.

Her heart ached for Radford. She wanted to go to him, wanted to hurry away from this place and return to his arms, but there was nowhere for her to go. She could not exactly climb out of the window, given that it was much too high up since they were on the second floor of the inn. Swallowing her tears, Elsbeth tried her best to think calmly, trying to come up with some way of escaping, only for her mind to refuse to do anything other than cry out for Radford.

A sharp rap on the door had her jumping and, as she turned her head, she saw the Duke step inside with a maid just behind him, carrying a gown in her arms.

"You are to eat, wash, and change," he said firmly, his eyes not so much as landing on her, as though she were so far below him he could not even allow himself to look at her directly. "Your groom will be here in a few hours."

Her heart stopped in her chest.

"Obviously, you cannot wear that," he continued, gesturing at her governess' gown with disdain. "The maid has all you require. I expect you to be ready within the hour."

Elsbeth stared at him, her mind slowly beginning to close in on itself as the truth hit her with such force that it took her breath away.

Her groom was coming here. The Duke's stepson, the heir apparent, was to arrive at the inn so that they might marry.

"I will not," she whispered, as the Duke made his way to the door. "I will not marry him."

"You will," the duke replied, in a tired voice as though growing irritated with her constant refusal. "I have the Special License and the local vicar has made himself available to me whenever I request his presence. Whether or not the words leave your mouth, this particular vicar will ensure that, by law, you are married to my stepson."

Elsbeth shook her head. "You cannot have me wed without my consent."

The Duke sneered at her, his eyes glinting from underneath his bushy eyebrows. "My dear lady, when will you learn that I can do whatever I wish?" He shook his head disparagingly. "After all, I am a Duke and, as such, can do whatever it is I desire with very little consequence. And so, Miss Blakely, it is quite ridiculous of you to even attempt to prevent this from occurring, for I can assure you that it will come to naught. You will be married, and you will return to my stepson's home as his wife. The rest, of course, is up to him. I pray that the heir will soon be in your belly and that my family line, tainted as though it may be by your presence, will continue."

Elsbeth lifted her chin, despite the quivering of her lips, determined not to quail under the steady yet malicious gaze of the Duke. "I will do no such thing. I am to wed Lord Radford. He will come for me."

The Duke's harsh laughter echoed around the room. "Then let us hope that thought continues to comfort you, Miss Blakely, for that is all it will do, I assure you." He shot a dark look towards the maid. "Within the hour, mind."

The maid, clearly terrified, bobbed a curtsy and

dropped her eyes to the floor, not looking at either Elsbeth or the Duke. The door slammed shut behind him as the whole room seemed to shake from the force of it, leaving Elsbeth feeling weaker than ever before.

Crumpling into her chair, Elsbeth gave into the tears that had been threatening for so long, her agony pouring out of her with such force that it was all she could do to remain seated, wanting to slide to the floor and curl into a ball of hopelessness and pain.

"I'm sorry, miss, but I need to have you washed," the maid whispered, coming over to her and putting a gentle hand on her shoulder. "There's fresh water in the jug."

Elsbeth could do nothing but sob, her heart breaking over and over as she realized the hopelessness of the situation. If her groom was to come here and if the vicar was as willing to bend for the Duke, then within an hour or so, she would be wed to a man she did not know and forced to bear his child. Her life with Lord Radford would be over, brought to a swift end by the Duke's determination.

"Please," the maid begged, now tugging gently at Elsbeth's arm. "I dare not cross him."

That was the worst of it, the fear that the Duke placed in so many hearts. Even now, Elsbeth felt her own heart begin to weaken and quail, as though it were tired of being strong for such a long time.

"It is of no use," she whispered to herself, refusing to move an inch. "He will have his way regardless."

The maid was young, with large frightened eyes that stared back at her as Elsbeth lifted her head. She was clearly upset by Elsbeth's tears, but fear of the Duke was forcing her to act anyway.

"I must dress you," the maid said again, growing almost frantic as Elsbeth refused to move. "I don't know what will become of me if I do not."

Elsbeth shook her head. "No. I will not do this."

"*Please,*" the maid cried, her own eyes now filling with tears. "The Duke, he....."

Looking up at her again, Elsbeth wiped her eyes and tried to focus on the girl in front of her.

"He's going to do you harm if you don't get me to do as he said," she finished, dully, aware that the Duke was doing all he could to force her to act. "Is that right?"

The maid nodded wordlessly, her eyes now swimming with tears. "Please, miss. It's not that I think he's doing the right thing, but I can't let him hurt my sister."

"Your sister?"

The maid nodded. "She's all I've got, my sister. She's a maid here too, although it's not the best place to work. I mean, the innkeeper keeps looking at us both with this gleam in his eye and it's all I can do to avoid him." She shuddered slightly, her cheeks pale. "We need to work, so it's not as though we can just go somewhere else, but the innkeeper's not a good man. He does what the Duke wants for enough coin – and so he put my sister in the Duke's room." She stifled a sob as a single tear dripped onto her cheek. "I have to get you changed and ready, else the Duke will....do something to her."

Her gut twisted with revulsion.

"Then there's nothing I can do but obey," Elsbeth muttered, finding the strength to push herself up out of the chair. "Here. I won't stop you." She turned around, the maid already beginning to unbutton her dress with such frantic fingers that Elsbeth could almost feel her fear.

"Is he forcing you to marry, then?" the maid asked, quietly. "I'm sorry to ask but –"

"Yes, he is," Elsbeth replied, as the gown fell to the floor. "Even though I am engaged to another."

Suddenly, out of nowhere, a thought hit her, hard. Turning around, she caught the maid's hand, her eyes widening.

"But it is to a good man, a kind man. A viscount."

The maid stared back at her, eyes widening.

"He would give you and your sister a position for life, I know he would," Elsbeth continued, almost frantic with hope. "If you were to help me, that is."

Blinking furiously, the maid began to shake her head, only for Elsbeth to catch her hand again.

"I do not mean to put you or your sister in danger," Elsbeth continued, quickly. "Do as the Duke asks and then, when I am ready, I will tell him that I need some time to pray. After all, getting married almost requires such a thing."

"And what should I do then?" the maid asked warily, her brows now furrowing.

"Take your sister and find a ladder," Elsbeth continued quickly. "There is one somewhere, surely?"

The maid nodded, her eyes widening with understanding.

"Put it to my window. I shall climb out and we will run away together."

"Run away?" the maid repeated, sounding both shocked and terrified. "I can't – I mean, what if the Duke....?"

"He will not find us," Elsbeth replied, with more certainty than she felt. "Besides, my betrothed, Viscount Radford, will protect you both. I promise you that. You will have employment for the rest of your life in our home, I can assure you of that."

Something flickered in the maid's eyes and Elsbeth felt her heart burst with hope.

"Please," she finished softly. "You are my only chance. You know what the Duke is forcing me to do. I cannot escape him without you."

After a long moment, the maid nodded slowly, her fear palpable.

"Very well," she said, even though her whole body was beginning to shake. "I – I'll try my best."

It was all Elsbeth could hope for, her eyes closing tightly as she fought off another wave of tears.

"Thank you," she whispered, putting one hand on the maid's shoulder as she tried to steady her composure. "What's your name?"

"Betty," the maid said, reaching for Elsbeth's gown. "And my sister's Mary."

"Then thank you, Betty," Elsbeth replied, praying silently that this would work. "Thank you for your courage."

. . .

Half an hour later and the Duke was back at her door. Elsbeth stood tall as the maid edged towards the door, her eyes fixed on Elsbeth.

"You can have your stinking sister back," the Duke snarled, as Betty made her way past him. "Not that I would have touched her, filthy creature." His lip curled as Betty went past him, her whimper of fear making its way back towards Elsbeth's ears.

"Your groom will be at your door very soon," the Duke continued, the moment Betty left them. "I am glad to see that you decided to do as you are told, for once."

It was on the tip of Elsbeth's tongue to say that she had not exactly had a choice in the matter, but she chose not to say a word, bowing her head instead. It was best not to anger him, to let him believe that perhaps, finally, she had learned her place.

"I will stay with you until he arrives."

Her stomach tightened.

"I must spend some time in prayer, your grace, before my husband to be arrives." She looked up at him, seeing the slight frown on his face and praying that he would leave her alone. "After all, this is quite a serious occasion, is it not?"

"It is," he murmured, still frowning.

"A few minutes is all I require," she continued, now dropping her gaze to the floor again. "It is not too much to ask, is it?"

There was a long, pronounced silence. Elsbeth held her breath, waiting for his judgement to fall. If he remained with her, then there was nothing she could do to escape, for her chance to climb out of the window and onto what she hoped to be the waiting ladder, would be gone.

"A few minutes," he said eventually, walking towards the door. "Your groom has not yet arrived and so I suppose I may grant you this." He chuckled softly. "After all, you will need all the prayer you can get if I know my stepson."

Elsbeth let out her breath slowly, her skin crawling as she tried not to dwell on what the Duke meant. She waited until the door closed and the key turned in the lock before hurrying to the window, throwing open the shutters and looking out.

There was no-one there. No ladder. Nothing. The light of the moon shone on the wall beneath her, making it plain just how far she would have to fall if she tried to jump.

Something hissed.

Jerking in surprise, Elsbeth looked down to the ground, only to see a few moving shadows, not quite sure what it was or where it had come from. A clattering sound made her wince, her stomach tightening as she worried that the Duke would hear it.

And then, to her relief, a ladder was placed against the wall just below the window, another hiss coming from the ground below.

Swallowing hard, Elsbeth pulled her head back into the window and turned around, bundling up her gown in one hand. How she managed to maneuver herself out of the window, she was not quite sure, although there was a sound of tearing as she managed to put one foot on the first rung of the ladder.

Sweat trickled down her back as she held onto the windowsill, barely aware of the scrapes burning on her skin. Drawing in a deep breath, Elsbeth began to climb carefully down the ladder, her hands tight on the wooden rungs as she made her way down.

And then, there came a wild shout. The sound of a door slamming open made her stop in fear, only for the voices of the two maids to force her into action. She clambered down the last few steps, her gown billowing around her in the wind as hands caught her around the waist.

"Hurry!" Betty whispered, as the other maid – the one Elsbeth presumed to be Mary – let the ladder fall to the ground. "This way."

Elsbeth did not have time to think, hurried away by the two maids as they made their way along the side of the inn. The shouts of the Duke were still ringing in her ears as she ran with Betty and Mary, terrified that a strong hand was about to grasp at her shoulder.

"Here," Mary whispered, shoving Elsbeth hard into a small, dark building. "They might not find us in here."

Elsbeth looked all about her but saw nothing but darkness, her breathing coming quick and fast.

"Where are we?" she whispered, as Betty led her around the back of something. "I don't understand."

Betty patted her hand, even though Elsbeth could feel her trembling. "This is where they keep the firewood," she whispered, coming to a stop and pulling Elsbeth down to the floor. "The pile's huge. Let's hope they won't look here."

Swallowing her fear, Elsbeth tried to smile into the

darkness. "Thank you for your courage, Betty. And you too, Mary."

A small sniff came from Mary's direction. "Betty says we got a job for life if we help you."

"Yes, of course you do," Elsbeth replied, firmly. "With a good man, too. Although, we just have to make sure not to be found first." She looked all about her but saw nothing but inky shadows. "Is there another way out of here?"

There was silence for a moment.

"There's a gap just behind me" Betty replied, eventually, as the shouts of the Duke and the sound of whinnying horses came ever closer. "It's small but you can fit through – but it doesn't lead anywhere. Just back out into the open."

Elsbeth swallowed hard, drawing in a long breath in an attempt to reassure herself. "Good. Then let's just pray that no-one comes to search for us here."

"What do we do when the morning comes?"

Elsbeth couldn't answer, her throat suddenly aching with a deep and terrible fear. She had no idea what to do if the Duke found her, aware that with first light would bring a greater chance of being discovered.

She tried to speak, but her lips refused to move, her mouth filled with sand. Her mind scrambled to think of an answer, but all she could do was shake her head.

"I don't know," she managed to whisper, eventually. "All I know is that, somehow, I've got to get home."

. . .

For a long time, there was nothing but fear prickling up and down Elsbeth's spine. She could hear the Duke roaring in anger, the sound of a man's voice that she didn't know, which Betty whispered to her was the innkeeper yelling at his servants to go in search of them.

"There ain't a lot of them," Mary whispered, pressing Elsbeth's hand as they sat together. "Those who work for the innkeeper, I mean. Not loyal, neither."

Elsbeth nodded in the darkness, hoping that this meant the men wouldn't be particularly willing to find them. Tears pricked at her eyes as she thought about Lord Radford, her arms wrapped around her knees in an attempt to keep out the chill that was settling into her bones.

And then, out of nowhere, she heard a familiar shout.

Her head shot up, her eyes widening in the darkness.

"It's him!" she breathed, her hands now scrabbling for Mary and Betty. "It's Radford!"

In her haste, she made to get up, only for Mary and Betty to grab at her and pull her back down.

"No," Betty hissed, fervently. "You can't. The Duke is still there."

Everything in Elsbeth wanted to go to the Radford, even though the Duke and his stepson were still there. Her body quivered with tension as she clung to Betty's arm, her ears straining to hear Radford's voice.

"Where is she?" she heard him yell, his voice shattering the darkness around her. "I know you brought her here."

The Duke exclaimed something that Elsbeth couldn't hear, whilst the mocking laughter of the stepson floated around them. Elsbeth felt herself grow hot all over, anger and fury filling her.

The Duke had always treated her as though she were something to be shifted about at his will. He had been the one to put her in the Smithfield House for Girls, just in case she should prove useful at a later time, and now, since she was the only one of his bloodline left, she was meant to simply marry a man and bear his child because the Duke willed it.

It was a feeling she'd rebelled against her whole life. The feeling of being told what to do, of being ordered about as though she had no choice of her own. When would the Duke see that she was not the kind of woman to be so mistreated?

Before she knew what she was doing, Elsbeth shook off Betty and Mary's hands and rose to her feet, walking out of the darkness and back towards the inn. She did not feel as though she were putting herself in danger, knowing that Radford was there waiting for her. He would protect her. Once she was by his side, she would have nothing to fear.

Slowly making her way back towards the inn, Elsbeth saw three figures standing in the moonlight. Two had their back to her, and, in the distance, she saw another strong figure. A figure she knew to be Lord Radford.

Drawing her skirts up in one hand and taking a deep breath, Elsbeth ran as hard as she could, taking a wide berth past the Duke and his stepson, before shouting Radford's name. In a moment, she was in his arms again, held tightly against him as he wrapped his arms around her waist.

"Elsbeth," he gasped, his breathing ragged with surprise. "Elsbeth!"

"Unhand her at once!"

Elsbeth held onto Radford tightly, her arms encircling his neck.

"You found me," she whispered, ignoring the Duke completely. "I couldn't let you look for me in vain. I had to be by your side." Loosening her grip a little, she looked into his eyes, seeing them alight with relief in the moonlight. "I knew you'd keep me safe."

"Always."

CHAPTER NINETEEN

Andrew could barely believe it. Elsbeth was finally back in his arms, having appeared out of nowhere. He had taken the road indicated to him by one of his men and had, after a few wrong turns, finally managed to make his way to the Winter Arms. He had jumped down from his horse just as the Duke had come storming out of the inn, a man he did not recognize by his side.

However, Andrew now realized that this was the Duke's stepson, Lord Drake, the man meant to marry Elsbeth. Both of them were advancing towards Elsbeth, clearly determined to take her from him by force.

"Stop!" he shouted, anger racing through his veins and setting his body alight. "Elsbeth is my betrothed. She belongs in my house. You are not to touch her."

Setting her a little behind him, Andrew took a step back towards his horse, grasping Elsbeth's hand behind his back and tugging it gently. He wanted her to go to the horse, to climb up and ride away if she had to, but the way her fingers curled around his told him that she was not intending to leave his side.

"You will leave her with me," the Duke replied, darkly, pulling something out from behind his back. "I have not come this far only to have her taken from me."

A soft click made Andrew stop dead, hearing a gasp of shock from Elsbeth.

"I believe my stepfather has made it quite clear," Lord Drake said, gruffly. "Hand her over."

"Never."

His voice was loud and determined, pushing all fear and doubt away. The Duke was not about to intimidate him with such a thing as a pistol. He was not about to simply step away from Elsbeth for fear that he might be shot. Andrew knew that he would protect her with everything he had, even if it meant giving away his last breath in her defense.

"And how would that look, do you think?"

Elsbeth stepped out from behind Andrew, her hand still in his. "The Duke of Broadshore, shooting an unarmed viscount?"

The Duke snorted. "As if anyone would believe your story."

"And what makes you think there are not others who would corroborate it?" Elsbeth asked, her voice ringing out in defiance. "I know for certain that the Dowager Viscountess would be able to talk of your threats towards her son, about the way you tore me from my home. Miss Amy, child though she is, can talk of the man who stood by my side when I asked her to go indoors."

Lord Drake laughed harshly, his voice so like that of the Duke's. "And who would believe a child? Many will believe that you went with the man willingly."

"How many would believe a Dowager, a child, the servants, the maids, the innkeeper and my own testimony?" Elsbeth asked, softly, no trace of fear in her words. "I assure you now that, should you continue with this fateful plan of yours, nothing but trouble will come after it."

There was a short silence. The first streaks of dawn were making their way across the sky and, as Elsbeth watched, she saw a flicker of concern in Lord Drake's face.

"Your grace, perhaps –"

"Get out of my way!"

The Duke advanced on them both, as Andrew put himself directly in front of Elsbeth once more. Taking his eyes away from the man, he turned towards Elsbeth, seeing the fear in her gaze as she watched the Duke.

"Climb on the horse and ride home from here," he whispered, squeezing her hand. "Please, Elsbeth. I must know you are safe."

She shook her head. "No. I will not leave you."

"You must."

Her lips trembled as she tried to shake her head no, only for the Duke's shout to startle her into action. With a sigh of relief, Andrew felt her go, only for the furious face of the Duke to come into his vision.

With a hard shove, Andrew pushed the older man back, far too aware of the pistol still held in his hand. He heard the horse whinny, praying that Elsbeth was already astride, as he grasped for the pistol. The Duke screamed in fury, his eyes wide as he tried to fight for the pistol – and all the while, Lord Drake stood silently, unmoving.

The Duke, despite being an older man, was stronger than Andrew had expected. It did not help that he managed to strike Andrew hard across the face, sending him spiraling into the dirt. Dazed, he heard the Duke shout for Lord Drake to go after Elsbeth and, struggling to get to his feet, Andrew tried to move forward to stop him from doing so.

Everything was moving slowly. Andrew could barely see in the early morning gloom, his vision blurring as he staggered to his feet. From his right, he could see the Duke shouting and gesturing into the darkness, clearly unable to go running after the horse himself, whilst Lord Drake was on his left, only now beginning to move.

Andrew did not hesitate. He knew he had to give Elsbeth as much time as she could to get away, so, despite the pain in his head, he jumped at Lord Drake, intending to tackle him to the ground.

A gunshot sounded, just as he moved. Something tore past his side, burning his skin, only for Lord Drake to scream aloud and fall heavily to the ground.

Then everything became very still.

Andrew shook his head in an attempt to clear his vision, bending on hands and knees as he tried to make sense of what happened. The Duke was silent, Lord Drake said nothing, and even the dawn chorus of birds seemed to have been startled into silence.

"Drake!"

The word was more of a moan than a cry, and slowly,

as Andrew turned his head, he realized that Lord Drake was now bleeding from a wound to his shoulder. The Duke, the pistol now lying uselessly in his hand, collapsed by his stepson's side, looking down helplessly at the blood.

"Here."

Andrew didn't know what he was doing, or why he was helping the man, but tearing the coat from his back, he threw it over Lord Drake and instructed the Duke to press down at the wound.

"I do not think he will die," he said, somehow managing to get to his feet. "But you will need a doctor."

It was only then that he realized that the bullet had burned a line across his ribs before going into Lord Drake. Because Andrew had been trying to get the man on the ground, the bullet had hit them both at different angles. Closing his eyes for a moment, Andrew drew in a ragged breath, trying to battle the waves of pain that were now shooting through his body.

"Radford!"

Elsbeth jumped down from her horse and came running towards him, her face sheet white in the early morning dawn.

"I am all right," he promised, seeing how her eyes were drawn to the blood seeping through his shirt. "Just a scratch." Despite the pain, he took her into his arms again, holding her tightly. He felt her begin to weep, her tears dampening his shirt.

"It is all over now, I promise," he whispered, one hand pressed lightly against the back of her head as he closed his eyes, breathing her in. "We can return home. You need not fear the Duke again."

"I did not ever want to be a duchess," she whispered in his ear, her sobs slowly abating. "I would have given up everything for you, Radford. I only ever wanted to be by your side."

"And you shall always be there," he promised, suddenly desperate to have her as his wife. "We should go now. My mother and Miss Amy will be worried."

Letting go of him for a moment, Elsbeth looked back to where the Duke and his son were lying, aware of the innkeeper now hurrying towards them. "What happened?" she asked, as the Duke began to give frantic instructions to the innkeeper. "I don't understand."

Andrew shook his head. "He tried to stop me and shot the one person he actually has some consideration for," he replied, heavily. "Lord Drake did not appear to be as convinced as the Duke as to what he was meant to do, at least. I do not think that either of them will ever come near you again." Anger knotted in his stomach. "Although I should like to pay him back for what he did to you, Elsbeth. Goodness, I very nearly lost you." The frustration in knowing that the man was a Duke and, therefore, able to do almost anything he wished, began to run all through Andrew, tension burning into each muscle of his body.

"I do not want to ever consider him again," Elsbeth replied, as two figures detached themselves from the back of the inn and began to come towards them. "I think this is punishment enough, Radford. To have injured his own stepson, to have been denied the one thing he sought – I shall be content with that punishment, I think. I will not allow it to hang on me any longer. Instead, I will look to our future with happiness and joy, refusing to allow the dark parts of my life to send their long shadows over it."

Andrew looked back at her, his eyes meeting hers and, as he saw the smallest of smiles on her face, felt his own frustration and irritation begin to die away. She was right. He had to look to the future and forget the past, leaving the Duke and his stepson to their own choices in life. He would be content with Elsbeth, would spend the rest of his days trying to bring joy and laughter to their life together.

"Then shall we return home, together?" he asked, softly. "I am sure the innkeeper has a hackney we can make use of."

Elsbeth smiled at him, although the concern did not leave her face as he leaned on her, the pain from the bullet still coursing through him. "I have never had a home before, Radford, but I know that I have found one with you." She tipped her head as two maids came towards them, both looking rather hesitant. "And we shall have two more maids in our home too, Radford."

"Two maids?"

Andrew listened carefully as Elsbeth quickly sketched out the details of what had happened, his gratitude growing all the more.

"Of course, you shall have a place with us," he said at once, reassuring them both. "For the service you have provided my betrothed, I can never thank you enough."

And so, within the hour the hackney set off for Radford Estate. Andrew leaned back in his seat with

Elsbeth by his side, her head resting on his shoulder as he wrapped one arm around her. His heart was full, relief and love sweeping all through him. Finally, he had his beloved back in his arms, never to be parted from him again. He could not wait to make her his bride.

EPILOGUE

"That was a beautiful wedding."

Elsbeth sighed happily to herself as the Dowager pressed one gentle hand on her shoulder.

"I am very glad to have you as my daughter in law – and the new Viscountess Radford," the Dowager continued, gently. "Thank you for all you have done, Elsbeth. I have never seen my son as happy as he is today."

"I feel much the same," Elsbeth replied, feeling as though she were almost glowing with happiness. "After what we went through together, I believe nothing can ever break us apart."

"Nor do I."

Turning her head, Elsbeth smiled softly as her new husband, Lord Andrew Radford, walked into the drawing room and slipped one arm around her waist. He was more handsome than she had ever seen him, his eyes warm and filled with love. A sigh of contentedness escaped her as she leaned against him, safe in his arms.

"And you have heard nothing from the Duke?" the Dowager asked, as Andrew shook his head. "What a terrible man he is."

"The last I heard from my steward, Lord Drake is at home recuperating and intends to go to London for the season next year," he replied, with a small shrug. "No-one has heard from or seen the Duke. I would suspect that he is back at his estate, trying to keep himself away from any rumors that might start up from what happened."

Elsbeth shuddered despite herself, recalling with a little too much clarity the last time she had looked into the Duke's eyes. He had turned from where his stepson lay on the ground to look into her eyes as she'd made her way towards the hackney, and she had grown chilled by what she'd seen there. There was such malice, such hatred and yet, such anxiety over what he'd managed to do. Elsbeth had known then that he would not come after her again, would not dare to do so after what he had inadvertently done in injuring Lord Drake. She had not felt any sadness for him, nor any regret. Instead, she felt as though he had brought such a calamity upon himself.

"I do not mean to upset you," Radford murmured, his arm tightening around her waist. "Forgive me."

She smiled and shook her head. "It is forgotten," she replied, quickly. "And now that we are wed, I can look forward to our life here together."

"Which will start the moment we return from our honeymoon," Radford declared, as the Dowager smiled at them both. "Come now, my dear. The carriage is waiting."

Feeling as though she might burst with delight,

Elsbeth pressed a kiss to the Dowager's cheek, only for Miss Amy to come running into the room, caught up with the delights of the wedding day. Laughing, Elsbeth managed to kiss her cheek also, eliciting a promise from her to be on her very best behavior for the Dowager. She had no doubt that Miss Amy and her grandmother would get along very well and was already looking forward to returning to them both. To be a mother to Amy instead of a governess would be a challenge indeed, but it was one she was looking forward to.

"I cannot wait a moment longer," Radford whispered in her ear, tugging her away. "Come with me, Elsbeth."

Blushing furiously, Elsbeth allowed him to lead her down the staircase and into the waiting carriage, pausing only to collect a small, paper wrapped parcel that she had specifically asked to be left for her. Ensuring that Radford did not see her do so, she stepped inside and, after only a few moments, then began to wave out of the window to the Dowager and Amy as the carriage began to roll away.

"Finally, we are alone," Radford smiled, looking over at her tenderly. "Are you happy, my love?"

"I am," Elsbeth replied, softly, picking up the paper wrapped parcel and, unfolding it, gently taking out a delicate amadis flower. "Here, Radford. Here is the flower you once asked to purchase from me."

His eyes widened and he stared at her for a moment, before taking it from her. "My goodness," he breathed, brushing one gentle finger down a delicate leaf. "The first time we met, was it not?"

It was as clear in her mind as though it had taken

place only yesterday. "It was," she murmured, smiling at him. "Although you were rather different back then."

He shook his head, his gaze lingering on the flower for a moment before his eyes drew up to her own. "My love," he murmured, setting the flower aside and pulling her over onto his seat as they made their way out of the gates. "I believe I called you 'a fair flower', did I not? Well, I must tell you, my love, that you are the most beautiful creature I have ever set eyes on. Fairer than any flower, more lovely and delicate than any bloom."

His eyes warmed as she ran one hand down his cheek, feeling her heart swell with love for him. Their wedding day had been wonderful, filled with laughter and happiness, but she had longed to be alone with her husband, longed to be able to whisper words of love to him that only he would hear.

"I have never loved anyone as much as I have loved you," he continued, his gaze softening. "My dear Elsbeth, whatever would have become of me if you had not turned me down in such a way the first time we met?"

She laughed softly, remembering how arrogant and proud he had been. "But you are not that man any longer, Radford, and I love the man you have become." Her lips curved with a smile as he pressed a kiss to her temple. "You have become everything to me and I love you with all of my heart."

His lips met hers in a gentle kiss, passion beginning to burn between them. "I love you, Elsbeth," Lord Radford whispered, one hand brushing down her cheek. "And I always will.

All is well that ends well. I am glad that Radford turned out to be a good guy!

Like this book? Try the next book in the series!
Saved by the Scoundrel Read ahead for a sneak peak!

MY DEAR READER

Thank you for reading and supporting my books! I hope this story brought you some escape from the real world into the always captivating Regency world. A good story, especially one with a happy ending, just brightens your day and makes you feel good! If you enjoyed the book, would you leave a review on Amazon? Reviews are always appreciated.

Below is a complete list of all my books! Why not click and see if one of them can keep you entertained for a few hours?

The Duke's Daughters Series
The Duke's Daughters: A Sweet Regency Romance Boxset
A Rogue for a Lady
My Restless Earl
Rescued by an Earl
In the Arms of an Earl
The Reluctant Marquess (Prequel)

A Smithfield Market Regency Romance
The Smithfield Market Romances: A Sweet Regency Romance Boxset
A Rogue's Flower

Saved by the Scoundrel
Mending the Duke
The Baron's Malady

The Returned Lords of Grosvenor Square
The Returned Lords of Grosvenor Square: A Regency Romance Boxset
The Waiting Bride
The Long Return
The Duke's Saving Grace
A New Home for the Duke

The Spinsters Guild
The Spinsters Guild: A Sweet Regency Romance Boxset
A New Beginning
The Disgraced Bride
A Gentleman's Revenge
A Foolish Wager
A Lord Undone

Convenient Arrangements
Convenient Arrangements: A Regency Romance Collection
A Broken Betrothal
In Search of Love
Wed in Disgrace
Betrayal and Lies
A Past to Forget
Engaged to a Friend

Landon House

Landon House: A Regency Romance Boxset
Mistaken for a Rake
A Selfish Heart
A Love Unbroken
A Christmas Match
A Most Suitable Bride
An Expectation of Love

Second Chance Regency Romance
Second Chance Regency Romance Boxset
Loving the Scarred Soldier
Second Chance for Love
A Family of her Own
A Spinster No More

Soldiers and Sweethearts
To Trust a Viscount
Whispers of the Heart
Dare to Love a Marquess
Healing the Earl
A Lady's Brave Heart

Ladies on their Own: Governesses and Companions
More Than a Companion
The Hidden Governess
The Companion and the Earl
More than a Governess
Protected by the Companion
A Wager with a Viscount

Christmas Stories

Love and Christmas Wishes: Three Regency Romance Novellas
A Family for Christmas
Mistletoe Magic: A Regency Romance
Heart, Homes & Holidays: A Sweet Romance Anthology

Happy Reading!

All my love,

Rose

A SNEAK PEAK OF SAVED BY A SCOUNDREL

CHAPTER ONE

"Can you go fetch some more ale from the cellar? Looks like we'll be busy tonight!"

Caroline Devonshire laughed aloud as Mrs. Beeson, the tavern owner, shook her head at one of the men who was clearly asking for more liquor, despite the fact that he could not even raise his head from where it lay on the table. Setting down her cloth, she moved through the door that led to their own private quarters and grabbed the wooden handle of the trap door that led to the cellar.

Tugging it open, Caroline found a candle and carefully made her way into the cellar, trying not to shudder at the thought of rats. She should have been used to such a thing by now, she told herself, given that she'd been going down into the cellar almost every night for so many years. In fact, she could still recall the first time Mrs. Beeson had shown her where to go and what to do. She'd been younger then, much younger, but the sight of all the barrels and supplies stored down below had astonished her.

"Liquid gold," she murmured, picking up a smaller keg and hoisting it onto her shoulder, wincing as the rough wood sent a splinter into her finger. That was what Mrs. Beeson had called it, all that time ago. She'd told Caroline that men would pay well for good ale and had told her sternly that she was never to water it down, as some of the tavern owners were inclined to do. Caroline had learned that the hard-working men of Smithfield Market would come to the Beeson Arms over any other tavern if they sold good quality ale for a reasonable price. It still astonished her just how much of it some of them could drink!

Sweat trickled its way down her back as she put yet another keg down. She had brought four up from the cellar now, and surely that would do! Sighing to herself, she paused for a moment or two, simply to catch her breath. It was hard work here in the tavern, even though she was profoundly grateful to Mrs. Beeson for all she had done for her. Sometimes it just became rather wearying, having to force half-drunk men to leave the tavern, wincing as they tried to paw at her on their way out. They usually got a hearty slap from Mrs. Beeson if they tried such a thing, although Caroline hadn't quite yet managed to raise a hand to anyone. She preferred to use strong words to make her point, which, for the most part, seemed to work. It was only when some of the men were so far in their cups that they seemed to have lost the ability to listen that she became a little more intimidated.

"Thank goodness for Martin," she murmured to herself, picking up one of the kegs and carrying it back through to the front of the tavern. Martin was a new addition to the tavern, hired by Mrs. Beeson to ensure that she and Caroline were never in danger. Mrs. Beeson had said that it was simply because she'd become a little older these last few years and needed a man's strength to help her move some of the men when it came to closing time, but Caroline suspected it was also due to the fact that she was now of age. Mrs. Beeson had always been a protective figure in Caroline's life, ever since she'd come to the Beeson Arms, and for that, Caroline was profoundly grateful. Even now, even though she was safely behind the counter, Caroline was glad to know that Martin was nearby, watching everyone through those dark beady eyes of his. He would be ready to step in, in case things became a little too rowdy. Deep down, Caroline hoped that Mrs. Beeson and Martin might one day, perhaps, marry, for she had seen the way that they looked at one another – although she had not said as much to Mrs. Beeson, of course. Mrs. Beeson had been on her own ever since her husband had died and left her the tavern some ten years ago now, which had been around the same time that Caroline had come into her life. They'd worked in this tavern together, had worked hard to build it up and make it the best tavern in Smithfield Market. That hard work had paid off. Caroline smiled to herself as she put another keg down behind the counter, hearing the loud conversations all mixing together above her head as the men talked loudly about all kinds of things. Someone was singing, although she had no idea who it was or what song they were attempting. As she laughed, she heard someone else join in too, although they appeared to be singing an entirely different song.

"Thank you, Caroline," Mrs. Beeson said, bustling over to her and handing her the cloth. "Clean up the counter, will you? That Mr. Johnston's gone and spilled his glass everywhere and you know what I say about the counter!"

Caroline smiled at Mrs. Beeson, seeing the sharpness of her eye as she glared at Mr. Johnston, who had gone a slight shade of red. Mrs. Beeson was shorter than Caroline, with strong arms and back that told everyone who saw her that she wouldn't accept any kind of nonsense from them. Her long black hair was always twisted up neatly into a bun. Lately, Caroline had spotted one or two silver hairs threading amongst the black. She had a square jaw, a strong nose, and dark brown eyes that didn't miss a single thing. Whilst Caroline had heard Mrs. Beeson complain that she was not in any way a handsome woman, to her, Mrs. Beeson had such a beauty in her character that it did not matter how she looked. Her kind heart, her goodness, and her fierce determination to do all she could to look after Caroline meant so much to Caroline that she felt as though she were never able to express it. She worked hard, day in and day out, with the tavern only closed on Sundays, as expected. Mrs. Beeson had taught Caroline everything she knew about this life. In return, Caroline was determined to work as hard as she could so that the Beeson Arms would continue to do well.

"I'll get right to it," Caroline replied, picking up the cloth and going to rinse it in the bowl of water behind her. "Is there broken glass?"

Mrs. Beeson shook her head. "No, thank goodness,

but there's a stack of glasses and tankards that'll need washing."

Caroline bit back a groan, trying her best to nod and smile.

"Thank you, Caroline," Mrs. Beeson murmured, now looking a little less frustrated. "I don't know what I'd do without you."

Plunging the final glass into the bowl of now lukewarm water, Caroline scrubbed it thoroughly before setting it aside, knowing that she would have a great many more drinking vessels to wash before the night was through. This was the one chore she hated the most, simply washing the dirty pewter tankards or glasses over and over again. Picking up her cloth, she began to dry them, whilst keeping a close eye on the men she could see through the open doorway that led back into the tavern itself. Mrs. Beeson was doing a fine job on her own, as she always did, making sure that the men who asked for more ale got what they wanted. Caroline knew she wouldn't always give them a full glass depending on the state they were in. She was good that way, Caroline thought to herself, knowing that Mrs. Beeson was both honest and kind-hearted. She never gave a man half a pint and charged for a full one, even though some were so drunk that they wouldn't have noticed. There was something about working in Smithfield Market that made everyone a little more aware of each other, as though they knew they were expected to look out for one another. That was what Mrs. Beeson did and it was what she had instilled in Caroline. If a man was drunk, then he'd struggle to get up in time for work in the morning, and if he didn't get to work in the morning, then he might be dropped from his employment and that would mean no more money. Money that he would use to feed, clothe and house not only himself but his family. It was, as Mrs. Beeson had said so often before, her responsibility to ensure that didn't happen. A man in his cups wasn't able to remember to take that responsibility for himself, and so would demand more and more ale – but Mrs. Beeson would always refuse to give it to him, no matter how much he asked.

That was probably why they had such a good reputation, Caroline mused to herself, setting down another dry glass. The men knew that Mrs. Beeson would never let them give in to the worst of themselves.

The door to the tavern opened and in came another three or four men. Caroline shook her head, a half smile on her face. It was late enough already and here these men were looking for something to drink when, most likely, they ought to be thinking about heading on home to their families. Mrs. Beeson would get them a couple of drinks, of course, but within the hour, she'd be taking last orders and then closing up the tavern until the morrow.

"And then I can head to bed," Caroline murmured to herself, stifling a yawn. She always grew tired this time of night, when it drew near to closing time. All she had to do was keep on going for just a little longer.

"Miss Devonshire?"

Looking up, Caroline saw one of their regular patrons standing framed in the doorway, leaning heavily against it.

"Mr. Moorside," she said, firmly, with only a small

smile on her lips. "You know very well you're not meant to be back here."

He chuckled low in his throat. "But how can I stay back there when I know you are in here?"

She shook her head, letting out a long breath as she sighed inwardly. This was one of the downfalls of working in a tavern.

"Mr. Moorside, I know full well that you are married with a couple of children under your roof and I'm not the type to go after a man such as that."

He didn't move, the smile lingering on his handsome face. "Is that so?"

"It is," she said firmly, wondering why she had to tell this man the same thing every few days. "But you know that already, Mr. Moorside."

The smile stretched even further on his face, making him look a little like a jack in the box as the shadows flickered across his features.

"But I'm a little lonely, Miss Devonshire," he wheedled, one eyebrow lifted. "You know that my wife's gone and got herself with child again and she doesn't want me in her bed."

Trying not to roll her eyes, Caroline planted both hands on her hips. "That means you should be taking care of your wife then, Mr. Moorside," she said sternly, "instead of just worrying about your own pleasures."

Mr. Moorside's smile finally began to fade and he shook his head in apparent dismay. "Does that mean you aren't amenable to my advances then, Miss Devonshire?"

"As before, Mr. Moorside," she stated, calmly. "You will find me unchanged in this. No, I do not care for any man's advances, no matter how kind or sweet they may try to be in encouraging me into their arms." She lifted one eyebrow, keeping her stance strong. "I do hope I've made myself clear."

The face of Mrs. Beeson appeared just behind Mr. Moorside, her eyes flashing suspiciously.

"Is everything all right here?"

Caroline rolled her eyes as Mr. Moorside jumped in surprise, turning to face Mrs. Beeson and managing to stagger just a little as he did so.

"Mr. Moorside, is there a reason for you being in the back of my establishment?" Mrs. Beeson asked, warningly. "I do hope you're not bothering my Caroline again."

Mr. Moorside held up his hands in supposed defense. "No, not at all, Mrs. Beeson. I was just talking to her, that's all. Thought she might be a bit lonely in here all by herself."

Mrs. Beeson narrowed her eyes. "Don't you worry about Caroline, Mr. Moorside. She's just fine as she is, isn't that right, Caroline?"

Caroline nodded, a wry smile on her face as she saw Mr. Moorside begin to stutter.

"I would hate to have to ban you from the Beeson Arms," Mrs. Beeson continued, a little coldly. "But any more of this, Mr. Moorside, and I'll do just that."

Mr. Moorside stammered an apology and quickly made his way back into the tavern itself, not even so much as looking back.

"Are you quite all right?"

Caroline smiled as Mrs. Beeson looked at her a little

anxiously, shrugging her shoulders. "I'm fine, Mrs. Beeson, thank you. Nothing I couldn't handle."

As she'd grown up, Caroline had become used to shooing away advances from the men who frequented the tavern. Some had become a little more lewd of late, but she'd managed to stop them in their tracks regardless. It helped that Mrs. Beeson kept an eye out for her. She knew that Martin would be on hand if things got ugly. The men always complimented her, which she knew was just to try and sweeten her up in the hope she might end up cuddling up to them. She shook her head, biting back a sigh. The men who came to the tavern were nothing like the kind of men she sometimes let herself dream about.

"You ought to be thinking about your future, Caroline," Mrs. Beeson said, interrupting Caroline's thoughts. "A tavern isn't much of a place for you."

Caroline smiled at the lady, knowing that Mrs. Beeson had expressed the very same thing multiple times before. "Mrs. Beeson, I'm quite happy here."

Mrs. Beeson shook her head. "This tavern is doing well thanks to you, but I don't want you to think you've got to stay here. I can hire a girl if you ever want to up and leave for a bit. Mind you've got that fortune from your parents!"

Caroline *did* remember but shook her head. It was not really a fortune although it certainly was a substantial amount of money and, for that, she was grateful. However, even though that money was now available to her since she had turned eighteen, Caroline had no idea what to do with it. She was well aware that, even if she did go in search of her own life for a time, she would eventually have to find employment for her monies would not stretch until the end of her days.

"You should be out exploring the world," Mrs. Beeson continued, gently. "Out meeting folk, finding someone to fall in love with you and make a new life for yourself. You don't have to stay here, Caroline. I don't want you thinking you're obliged to do that."

"I don't," Caroline replied at once, reassuring Mrs. Beeson. "For the time being, I'm quite happy here, Mrs. Beeson. This is my home. This is the only life I've ever really known and I'm truly grateful for it. Perhaps, in time, I'll start yearning for an adventure but there's nothing of that in me as yet. I'm happy here in Smithfield Market, really."

Mrs. Beeson did not look at all convinced, wearing a look that Caroline knew all too well to be an expression of slight disbelief, but she eventually shrugged, sighed and turned her back to go back into the tavern.

"It's your life, Caroline," she said, over her shoulder. "Just make sure you're doing whatever it is *you* want."

Caroline sighed to herself, shaking her head and muttering under her breath as she picked up another glass to dry. The truth was, she had very little idea of what it was she wanted to do with this life she called her own. With a brother away in the army and her parents long gone from this world, there was very little security for her other than in the Beeson Arms. Was it fear that held her back? Or was it that she truly did feel at home here?

Biting her lip, Caroline set the last glass down, hung

the cloth back on the peg and walked back into the tavern, ready to help Mrs. Beeson with the final round of drinks. The problem here was that she had very little time to think. She was always so busy, either clearing up the tavern from the night before or preparing it for the night to come. There was always work to be done, and very little time to have to herself, to allow her thoughts to come out into the light and to truly consider them. However, at some point, Caroline knew she would have to let herself think about what Mrs. Beeson had said. As much as she knew she would always have a home here, perhaps she did need to step out from Smithfield Market and find a life of her own. A life where she could make her own choices and chase after her own dreams.

"Caro!"

She started, the glass she'd been filling jerking in her hand. Only one person called her Caro. A person she had not seen these last three years.

"Caro! Here!"

She set the glass down carefully, wiping the moisture from her hand with her apron before looking up, hardly daring to believe it.

"Peter!" she exclaimed, seeing his handsome face and felt tears prick at the corner of her eyes. "Oh, Peter. You've come home!"

CHAPTER TWO

Peter was Caroline's older brother. A brother who had found her a house and a home with Mrs. Beeson when their parents had died all those years ago. They had both caught a fever and Peter, being a good few years older than she, had packed his and Caroline's things and left the house, promising her that they'd come back once their parents had recovered.

How he'd managed to persuade Mrs. Beeson to take them both in, Caroline never knew, but somehow, they'd ended up living there for a time. Mrs. Beeson had lost her husband only a few months prior and perhaps it was that suffering that had allowed her to welcome two children into her home. They had, of course, helped at the tavern from the first day they'd arrived. Caroline could still recall how Peter had warned her that she needed to earn her keep. They'd done all they could to help Mrs. Beeson. Caroline had dreamed of the day when they would be able to return home to their parents, longing to be in her mother's arms again. But one day Peter came to her, sat her down and told her, in halting tones, that their parents had both succumbed to this mysterious illness.

She'd been so young then, hardly able to take it in, but yet she'd cried so hard and for so long for the mother she'd never see again.

And then, Mrs. Beeson had stepped in. Sometimes when Caroline closed her eyes, she could still remember the feeling of being wrapped in Mrs. Beeson's arms as she'd rocked her in the rocking chair by the fire, letting Caroline cry out all of her pain and grief. Mrs. Beeson had cried too, over the loss of a husband she'd loved, and perhaps it was that grief that had begun to grow the strong bond that was now between them.

Mrs. Beeson had become the mother Caroline had lost, although of course, she could never truly be replaced. From that day on, Mrs. Beeson had declared that Caroline and Peter were to consider the tavern their home, promising never to throw them out on the street or to send them to the poorhouse. Caroline was still grateful to this day for Mrs. Beeson's generosity, knowing that there was now a love between them that would never break apart. When Peter had left to join the army, Mrs. Beeson and Caroline had clung together and tried not to cry, both proud and afraid for him. Whilst Caroline's parents had never been nobility, they had worked hard and had built up a decent fortune for their two small children, a fortune that would have been all the larger had they lived, but Peter had used his share to purchase colors for himself when he turned eighteen. He was now a lieutenant in the cavalry, and whilst Caroline had been extraordinarily proud of him, she had always had the same familiar worry lingering in her thoughts. What if she was to lose a brother as well as her parents? Then she would be all alone in the world, with no blood relatives to call her own.

And now, here he was back with her again, his broad smile and bright flashing eyes so familiar to her.

"Peter!"

She ran around the counter and threw her arms around his neck, tears spilling from her eyes as she did so. He looked almost the same as she remembered him, although she swore he was taller and broader than before. His shock of dark brown hair was, as usual, entirely in disarray and his blue eyes – so similar to her own - were sparkling with delight.

"Oh, Peter!" she heard Mrs. Beeson exclaim and stepped aside to allow the lady to wrap her arms around him, seeing her just as tearful as she. "We have missed you."

Peter pressed a kiss to Mrs. Beeson's cheek. "I've missed you as well. It's good to be back home."

"You look so very handsome in your military uniform," Mrs. Beeson said, proudly. "Just imagine! My ward, a lieutenant!"

Caroline smiled as Peter wrapped one arm around her shoulders, feeling herself almost burst with happiness. He tugged at a stray curl that escaped from her bun, making her laugh. She had not seen her brother for a few years and yet now that he was here, it was as if they'd never been apart.

"Working hard as usual, are you Caro?" he asked, as

they walked together towards the counter. "This place seems busier than I remember it."

Glad to be able to get her brother a drink, Caroline laughed and made her way around to the back of the counter. "That's because Mrs. Beeson does such a good job of making this the best tavern in all of Smithfield Market!"

Mrs. Beeson chuckled as the conversation in the tavern began to grow to a loud buzz again, now that the interest in Peter's arrival had calmed down.

"Are you staying here tonight, Peter?" Mrs. Beeson asked, one hand on his shoulder.

He shook his head. "I'm on leave from the army for a bit – nothing serious, though. They just want us hard working men to have a bit of rest before we go back, you see, so I should be in town for a while. But I'm going to be staying with a friend."

Caroline was surprised, looking over at her brother as she served him his ale. "A friend?" Peter had never introduced her to any of his friends before and had always stayed at the tavern when he had been home on leave.

"He'll be here in a few minutes," Peter said, with a broad smile. "I do hope you'll like him, Caro. He's a good sort."

"Oh?" Caroline smiled as her brother drank his ale thirstily. "Can I get you another?"

He chuckled. "Please. And one for Brandeis."

She filled two glasses. "And is Brandeis in the army too?"

Peter nodded. "He's actually Lord Timothy Brandeis, second son to the Marquess of Fareshire."

That made Caroline stop in her tracks, her stomach twisting itself into a sudden knot. "He's of the nobility?" This was not a place where nobility ever came in, for it was much too below them. "I do not want him to think lowly of you, Peter, in coming here."

Peter waved a hand. "Brandeis is not like that, Caro, don't worry. He's a decent chap, really. Being in the army tends to blur the lines between nobility and the rest of us." He chuckled. "He'll like you, I'm sure."

That did not sound particularly endearing to Caroline, despite the fact that her brother clearly thought it should. She knew all too well the reputation of the gentlemen in the *beau monde*, hoping that Peter had not become unduly influenced by this Lord Brandeis.

"And you're to stay with him?" she asked, tentatively. "You will come and see me though, won't you?"

Peter looked surprised, his expression softening. "Of course I will, Caro. You were the first person I came to see since I got back to London last night. Just because I'm staying in town doesn't mean that I won't be here. I'll come by every night for dinner if you like."

Feeling a little better, Caroline smiled. "You don't have to do that, Peter. Not every night."

"Then definitely on Sunday's," he said, patting her hand. "I know that's your only day off and I do want to make sure I get to spend some time with you."

Her smile broadened. "That would be wonderful, and I know Mrs. Beeson would appreciate it too." She arched a brow, her expression growing a little wry. "Although imagine that, you getting to stay in a fancy townhouse! What's become of my ragamuffin brother?"

Chuckling as he grinned at her, Caroline shook her head, hardly able to believe it. "Friends with a lord," she muttered, as Peter laughed aloud. "My goodness, Peter. How things have changed!"

Peter made to say more, only for the door to the tavern to open again and a gentleman to walk through. Caroline's eyes went to him at once, taking in his rather overwhelming presence. He was tall with broad shoulders and a strong stance as he surveyed the tavern. His fair hair glowed in the candlelight and, as he turned his gaze onto her, Caroline felt herself grow a little weak with a strange rush of desire.

Catching herself, she dropped her gaze from the gentleman and made to pick up a few dirty glasses, warning herself not to become caught up in nothing more than appearance.

"Brandeis!"

Peter called out and got to his feet, beckoning the gentleman over. His uniform told Caroline that he was of higher rank than her brother, but that did not seem to make any difference to them given the way they greeted one another.

"Good to see you again, Peter," the gentleman said, with a broad smile. "I confess it took me a bit of time to find this place but I'm glad I managed to do so in the end, especially when I am greeted by such a pretty face."

Caroline felt her face flame as Lord Brandeis turned his face towards hers, clearly trying to flatter her. She did not look at him and, in fact, moved towards the man at the other end of the counter who was calling her name. Pouring him a glass of ale, she heard Peter explain to

Lord Brandeis that she was, in fact, his sister and to be careful where she was concerned.

What happens next for Caroline, Peter, and Lord Brandeis? Check out the rest of the story in the Kindle store Saved by the Scoundrel

JOIN MY MAILING LIST

Sign up for my newsletter to stay up to date on new releases, contests, giveaways, freebies, and deals!

Free book with signup!

Facebook Giveaways! Books and Amazon gift cards!
Join me on Facebook: https://www.facebook.com/rosepearsonauthor

Website: www.RosePearsonAuthor.com

Follow me on Goodreads: Author Page

You can also follow me on Bookbub!
Click on the picture below – see the Follow button?

Rose Pearson

Made in the USA
Coppell, TX
24 September 2022